In the Wine Press

Short Stories

Joshua Hren

In the Wine Press

Short Stories

 Angelico Press

First published in the USA and UK
by Angelico Press
© Joshua Hren 2020

For information, address:
Angelico Press
169 Monitor St.
Brooklyn, NY 11222
angelicopress.com

ISBN 978-1-62138-532-5 (pb)
ISBN 978-1-62138-533-2 (cloth)
ISBN 978-1-62138-534-9 (ebook)

Cover painting by Michael D. O'Brien, 1991
Cover Design: Michael Schrauzer

CONTENTS

Acknowledgments

"Horseradish" in *Clarion*, nominated for a Pushcart Prize, 2019

"Old Blood" in *The Agonist*, 2020

"Some Other Exit" in *Windover*, 2019

"Pawned" in *Cobalt*, 2017

"Their Fire is Not Quenched" in *Windover*, 2019

"A Little Bank in My Soul," finalist in the 2018 *Adelaide* Short Story Award

"Sick at the Thought" in *Adelaide*, 2017

"The Dead Letter Office," in a different form, in *Front Porch Republic*, 2020

"Tears in Things" in *Dappled Things*, 2019

"Proof of the Immortality of the Soul, with Reference to Beeswax Soap" in *Dappled Things*, 2009

The world is like a . . . press: under pressure.
—St. Augustine, *Sermones*

. . . this logarithm of all suffering, seemed,
though unmentioned, to hang fog-like
just over the room's heads, to drift between
the peristyle columns and over the decorative
astrolabes and candles on long prickets and
medieval knockoffs and framed Knights of
Columbus charters, a gassy plasm so dreaded
no beginner could bear to look up and name it.
—David Foster Wallace, *Infinite Jest*

For my children,
With awe and ache over what you will inherit

Horseradish

After such knowledge, what forgiveness?
—T. S. Eliot, "Gerontion"

EARLIER THIS EVENING, when cold-blooded clouds still walled off the sky, my dad and I leaned against the uneven railing of our second floor porch, the one we built together way back. The one that "balances on two rickety legs like a low-budget circus act on stilts." Or, that's how he puts it, never a grudge or rib-nudge reminding that it was my own unsteady hands made the thing come out rickety. His hot whispers, punctuated by "Money!" and "God help us all," sent spittle against the wall as he cranked at the old bolt. I sprained my back helping him peel away the gray tape that covered the cracks around the frame to keep the heating bill down. Unlocking and heaving open the door that led to the porch, Dad gave a smirk.

"This better be good," he said.

We had been watching talking heads interpret reality and argue interminably, had been taking turns kicking the floor to tip the antennae, shift the picture into focus, when the weatherman told us to get outside and see the comet. I suggested the porch and my father, down-to-earth as he is, said, "What's the big deal? It's a comet. Twenty some feet aren't going to matter an inch."

But, half an hour later, there we were, our bodies closer than they had been in years, herded together by the chipped boards he and I had measured and sawed and covered in several coats of a standard white some twenty years earlier.

When the overcast, cowing clouds continued to mosey, grazing slowly across the sky, when Dad's cocked gaze set off the swell of muscle and nerve that writhed in his neck, when the comet didn't come, or, if it came, it did so secretly or beyond what our perched eyes could see, he started jumping up and down in place. I was onto him. He had left his greasy gray sweatshirt on the living room floor, where it kept warm the cancerous laminate.

(*Actually* cancerous, not metaphorically so, as when we say "cancerous" to mean "eye sore" or something. The floor possessed all the grainy beauties of genuine wood, but it was coated with dubious chemicals whose names I cannot pronounce. Dad, who was keeping it while awaiting the verdict of a class-action lawsuit involving a Dutch lumber company based in China, brought the toxic faux floor up regularly, mostly as a joke along the lines of "Watch where you step, we're all gonna die!" Not long ago I came home to find Dad bent over one of the punitive planks, fumbling through a tangle of mom's poorly-molded plastic rosaries. In the half-light where he was undoing the knots glow-in-the-dark, flesh-colored Christs emitted a neon green aura that lit up his heavy face. He wiped something from his face and struggled to stand. "You kids do an old man the kindness of ringing the doorbell?" As Dad stood, a badly-nailed board flipped up and clacked his knee. "Well," he said, "we're so far in debt if I die by floor-boards is about the only way you'll have an inheritance. Not a bad one. A nice one, even.")

Anyway. Anyway, here we were waiting for the comet, etcetera. Dad was wearing only the same V-neck T-shirt he'd worn for decades, in the evenings, shedding as he did his formal work clothes as a falsely-accused prisoner puts off the old orange on the day of release, so that, it being November and not far from freezing, he could cut inside after a couple minutes, and I'd having nothing to say about that, it being incumbent upon humankind to pity the chilly.

So I stalled. I brought up one of those old sores that still burns but tickles too. I asked him if he remembered when he grounded me for dressing up like the Statue of Liberty and using my torch to light the crown on fire. I spoke of the memory as though it would have been natural for him to forget it, as though, in the heap of juvenile pranks and delinquent pleas for help, this one could have been misplaced or lost entirely. How, at six a.m. the morning after he grounded me, face covered in an expired pain cream, I drew upon the unfailing wisdom of those grim fairytales Babica read me through her belly-laughs, tying my sheets together and then anchoring one end to the bed leg while I lowered myself out the window. More farcical fairytale than finesse, I fell another ten feet from where the sheet ran out, looking both ways through an awful flinch, amplifying the aspects of his portrait that made my father the wicked overseer, myself the young righteous in distress.

Then I took off, washing my face at an unclean gas station bathroom before picking up my work check at Maxwell's Meats (where each day after school I swept discarded animal fat into an incinerator and doused the floor with a mild bleach cleanser that smelled like the surgery ward of a hospital) and acquired other unpaid wages by stealing enough packs of cigarettes for smoking and selling to underage kids outside of Casimir Pulaski Middle-School. How this means of income seemed so right, so bright, as though it'd carry me into retirement. And then, pockets padded with the petty allowances of twelve-year-olds, I had enough bus fare to ride the whole routes all day. Winter did not force me to come shivering back home.

How Dad happened to see me boarding that bus on the way home from work. It must have been two hours he followed the slow, screeching, capsule of my escape, waiting for me to get off. And then, after a speechless car ride home, the duration of my incarceration increased without recourse to a defense attorney or even a plea deal.

"But," I said, still straining to see the comet, "No more sheet ropes for me! I had my friends bring a ladder and prop it to the edge of the old porch. *That* porch, *really* shoddy, way more ready-to-fall than this one. And there I went—off into the night. The first of some twenty times. Did y'know? D'you know, too, I'd be back at first light? You did, Dad, didn't you? Knew it all," and here I pried my hands from my pockets and felt them fold clumsily together. "But did you know I did nothing but walk and walk and walk? No sketchy parties. No secret drug dens. You must have or you would've stopped me, right?"

Or was it, I now wondered for the first time, that he knew that I knew that he knew, and this alone was a heavy enough hand upon me.

"You just didn't want Mom to die of tossing and turning, not knowing where her child was. I need to know." I assured, almost aching over my artifice, as my wife and I couldn't, in conscience, bring children into this world: "Maybe Soph and I'll have a little one. Who'll turn into a big one. Couldn't bear it if we end up with our own runaway, God help us. But of course ours'll inherit all my sins. How—what does a parent do when that happens? Why didn't you beat the crap out of me when I defied you? Why'd you unlock the door in the middle of the night? Why let me in without letting me in? All'd you did was stay silent for a month, make me do some 'community service.' How does a parent know how to punish their kids? All I did was refinish those chairs and table for Mrs. Wojtik. It'd be a stretch to call it punishment. Can still feel the sawdust between my fingers."

I pried a crumb of wood from the rotting railing and held it up against the moon.

"The world in a grain of sand! And"—the moon waxed yellow—"the lemon-lacquer. I *loved* that work. Good work. Should have kept doing it. Shouldn't have fled when I showed up at the carpentry apprenticeship class without a toolbox. I let that foreman's know-it-all face scare me away."(A fat face that first smiled down on us apprentices and then snapped into a snarl, trained to be hungry for failure. Hard to blame him given the turnout. Future foremen and splinter-pricked saps. Wheat and chaff.)

"Wished I hadn't showered or something. Wished I had the lacquer on my hands still. *See, I can do what you do.* But I couldn't. Though I could've—you yourself showed me so much, how to fix things. And now what, another sham liberal arts BA doing work that a rat could if well-trained."

He looked at the floor as though little marbles from my mind had scattered there and were rolling in disparate directions. He looked at the porch door, left open slightly, and extended his wiry-haired, fungal-toed, slipperless foot, and shoved it open. Walking in he paused, asked over his shoulder:

"You remember when we were camping, the four of us, at Kettle Moraine? When was that? You remember? When we moved into this house. And you had your friends do your paper route but forgot to leave them the carrier-bags—those dirty ones you never cleaned, you crazy kid. They brought that old ladder out and lifted it up to the porch to 'break in' to our house. And by the time they came out with the bags some half hour later... I still don't know where in the high heck you stored those things to make it so hard on them... the cops were there, waking the neighborhood at six a.m. on a Sunday morning. How a boy from the Slovenian Ghetto ever ended up in a neighborhood like this, where three squads come for horseplay, don't ask," he said.

(The "Slovenian Ghetto," by the way, was no solicitation of sympathy. It was the paradise he'd lost, the measure of everything that came after, which meant that all hours spent beyond it were profane—an east of Eden deferment. Disappointment. The Slovenian Ghetto was a point of pride. He lifted it regularly, daily even, like a wide flag, careful never to let its edges touch the tainted suburban grass with its weird fertilized green. In his mind he still was there. In his mind neighborhoods still mattered, and being without one, being, say, in the homogenous safety of a sprawl, was something near anathema.)

Dad dipped inside, reappearing in a breath, slippered and sweatshirted and holding the Easter basket that Babica had weaved of dried palms. He set the brittle thing on the tilting TV tray that had been banished to porch. Reaching into the egg-round basket and pulling out a hardened horseradish root, he held it high, looming it over me with his right hand so help him God as he took my right hand in his left. I looked at his laughless lips. "For what you've done! You want me to give you the wounds of *Jezus Kristus* or what?" he asked, stabbing the horseradish into my peeled-open palm. "Still it would be not enough," he said, spitting. "*It* would be not enough to cover all you did to us, to your *Mati,* especially, when you were young. (You are still young, Blaise.) *It* would be enough but *you* would not be enough," he said, shaking his head like a newly-widowed spouse unable to apologize for all the things left unsaid.

Then, cupping against the wind, he started the root on fire with a rusty Zippo that still shot blue-orange, tossed it in an incandescent arc into the little fenced garden that Mom and Babica had dug and tended for ten years until last. Ten years it yielded half our family's sustenance. The crispest cabbages turned into the softest stuffed *halupki*. The horseradish nailed into the firm November soil, between the tomato trellises and the little lifeless chicken cage that I'd failed to come and tend in spite of what I promised Babica as she pelted me with wry-smile pleadings from her deathbed. Immediately the fiery root snuffed out, hidden behind the smoke until it bloomed into a burning bush of bitter herbs, dangling nails of horseradish that hung ready for Babica's harvesting hands, ready to be minced and mixed with vinegar and eggs, all to be eaten solemnly during Holy Week, a little each day, each day a little taste of His pain as the mixture of Slovenian suffering lit up your nostrils and eyes, agonizing your whole mind with its pungent fire, reminding you of the Passion, cleansing sinus cavities of professing and doubting souls alike until Easter's relief: no more need to eat the horseradish but now drowning them in the dandelion wine and then hanging them out to dry for little feasts of penance peppered throughout the coming year.

But Babica was dead and Mom was sick and so who would do the harvesting, who the preparations, who the penances that seemed to me so archaic, arching as they did painfully backward to the Passover Seder—the five bitter herbs chewed in silence while some patriarch read the Haggadah. As though the Angel of Death hovered atop the copper *lestenec* that *dedek* made in the old country with his own fat and fireproof hands. As though they brought their devils with them, and their Savior too. As though they could smuggle such superstitions and expect them to take root in the New World.

But there it was, the bush, burning regardless, giving off the heaviest heat I'd ever felt, a kind that invites you into a sleep that will drowse away your most hated aches. I let it sear into my heavy-lidded eyes, felt a strange smile reshape my face.

He too stared at the burning bush, the porch creaked a little with his slunk, contemplative weight. I didn't dare ask if he saw what I did, lest the purging fires be outed as delusion. Stay, illusion. Slunk in a corner of the porch, he stood there like a pugilist luring me to other purpled memories, better things to fight for. (He and I used to box bare-fisted in the basement, unseen by *Mati*, though she saw the undeniable bruises later during my nighttime baths. And then they'd fight, Mom and Dad, throwing whistling whispers like punches across their cramped bedroom as I strained to hear through the wall what they said. As though to invert the natural order, he stopped boxing me when I turned thirteen.)

I understood his tactic of letting me punch on and on until I got tired of his duck and weave when I wanted to really talk (which is to say, when I wanted, and believe me when I say this, I really wanted to *fight*). After all, half the time we had talked in the last ten years I ended up raising my voice and hands and throwing big heap-fulls of my college-cooked, cock-eyed thoughts about how the world works, scattering so much straw around the house with surefire abandon. *See these truths, fools! See?* Once, when we sat there in silence, unable to dredge up a single non-controversial sentence, chewing and relishing the *klobasa*, I threw some salt and pepper shakers, the strangely unbreakable ceramic ones he'd thrown at the TV so many years before. Dad, saying nothing, picked up every single salt crystal and put it back in, giving me a penny wise wink and patting me on the shoulder before he went outside to smoke, sacrificial wisps exiting his cigarette end and reaching upwards toward God.

Here now, porch-bound, I watched the last thin plumes of the now drenched bush conjoin mid-air and bloom into a terrifying, several-headed angel who headed heavenward without pausing to explain.

"Shit, Dad. Tell me. Why'd you stop? Why, when I started to really act like a punk, didn't you paddle me once or twice, keep me tame. Show me. Really show me." Halfway through my sentence I spotted the comet. It descended, as far as my eyes could see, into our garden, this stray cat of the cosmos. Stunned by how close I was coming to conversing, really truly communing with Dad, I did not register the gravity, did not marvel. But there was no comfort in what came next.

The branches of the burning horseradish bush parted like fingers and caught the comet, couching its reckless, chaotic thrust, and crushed it into heatless elementary particles that fell like a crumpled clod of soil from a Babica's gardening hand. The bush stopped burning. And then it lit again, an orb of mandarin orange around an eye of lapis lazuli, though the blow had shaken the nails of fresh horseradish from its fingery branches and they lay there in the glow of the neighbor's security light, which the whole ordeal had set off.

There is no way Dad can dodge this one, I said to no one else. But he blinked like a man watching the grass grow. Stretching his lower back, scratching around a scar above his right eye, he said, "I should really get another can of All-White exterior," and picked at the exposed parts of the porch, where the glossed white gave way to rotted brown wood. Beautiful wood, really, after a little sanding. "This isn't just good wood," he went on. "It's impossible to find this kind—at least at a price I can afford. If we were to take the power sander to it. Nah. If we were to take a half a Saturday. Anyway, Blaise, it'd be some work, but not a lot. Not too much. Not more than we've been capable of in the past. And worth it," he said, smiling, his yellow incisors jutting out in all their glorious crookedness. "This house will be yours, you know. And unless that class action suit smiles on us soon you'll get the gift of an unpaid mortgage, too."

But what he was asking for wasn't the porch. That was easy enough to see. More like time, maybe, or, proud as it sounds, what he wanted was *me.* I wanted desperately to help him, to offer my body entirely, like Issac under Abraham's knife. I wanted to move back into my old room. Home. My wife and I were on stilts far less sturdy than those my father and I stood on. I had thrown our salt and pepper shaker and shattered the built-in stained glass that had been there since the house had been built. And, I wondered, remembering the tenacity of her "I despise you," repeated three times, maybe the window had been there *before* the house. I could see the stained window, dangling there in transcendent weightlessness, waiting for the house to be built around it, gathering light and giving it away again, brilliant. Beer bottle brown and sunflower yellow pieced into a roaring, sharp-angled star—a comet, you could say. Or, as Babica had once observed, "The center of the *kozmos*, that thing. *Spektaku-larno,* Blaise, can't you see you, thick-head? You don't even know. To have that kind of glory in the middle of your house. A star in the shape of the cross of Christ. My God—don't you see?"

"Mom's not doing any better?" I asked.

"She and I made it through a game of poker. A hand. It was hard though. She couldn't remember the rules. I let her win," he said, leaning too far over the railing. "She smiled when I put the penny ante in her hand. Those eyes, Blaise. All the beauties of France in a face."

"What's God doing with a woman like that? She spent her whole life waiting on these people without memories, with amnesias and dementias. Madness with nice names. How long? Since you were two, so, thirty years. And now she's. Well. What. It's like, what, I'm not superstitious but it's like if she caught what they had. At fifty two. That's far too young to forget who you are," he said, "It never happened to the old in our old neigh-borhood. It was easier to get sick there, I swear to you. We should have stayed there, I say." And he stood on his toes, trying,

I suspected, to scout out the high rise hospital she had been fre-
quenting as patient rather than nurse of late.

The bush, still bloomed, had stopped burning. Or never had
been aflame. (Though, once again I asked myself, how else to
explain? I'd done one dose of psilocybin mushrooms but that
was some ten years before. No. Not that. No.) Maybe Dad came
out here and talked to the bush regularly, so this was no big deal.
Or, maybe Dad was mad with God over Mom, doing to Him
what he did when someone said something he disapproved of.
He'd just stare at you as though you weren't there for fifteen
minutes until you disappeared, then get on with another nice
night of doing nothing at all. Not likely, not at all. Half the time
he seemed to be muttering Hail Marys under his breath. But...

Dad looked at me and I let him. I did not avert my eyes, did
not turn toward some suddenly-discovered, hackneyed novelty
to the left or to the right. Nor did I inch backwards and pick
away at some adolescent scab, hankering for melancholy memories. I looked at him and he let me. He did not avert his eyes, did
not turn toward some suddenly discovered, hackneyed novelty
to the left or to the right. Nor did he inch backwards and pick
away at the porch paint, brushing out benign memories and
planned projects that could protect us from this.

"Why I did not kick the crap out of you," he said, rushing his
palms up and down his arms, his forearm hair thicker than ever.
But relaxed, quitting all comet-watching pretenses. "You ask.
You like to ask questions," he said, matter of fact, not breathy—
without the burden I first read into it. "I should ask you what
you did to deserve the outing you got. Why you're here, out of
nowhere, wanting to sleep in your old bed like a little baby.
Strange, Blaise. You always are a strange soul. But I let you in the
house. I did not kick you out. Even though you came here without your wife. Without Sophia. But I didn't ask you where your

wife is. I just did what I do these nights, none of you kids coming round here anymore. Watched TV and worry the rosary and let you be."

(After he broke the family TV with salt and pepper shakers, the replacement was not forthcoming, not for over ten years. During that decade his sole comfort—which he made us keep our lips sewn shut about—was the scalding hot baths mom made for him in the evenings, especially hot when he was in late, slaving half-happily, half-wearily over an important client's car. Mom, wearing the smile of her wedding photograph, steeped seven tea bags in the baths, lavender and chamomile, and this is what we were to never tell, the sweet yellow flower smell sneaking under the bathroom door and into our little noses as we lay in wait for him to wrestle with us, his hands still reeking of that irremovable grease that still when I catch a whiff is more real than secret baths of heated lavender. Mom keeps some of the spent teabags, snagged from the trash, buried in some drawer, commemorating the only tenderness he ever let her show him. Soph laughs at my own nostalgia—a grease-drenched wrench Dad gave me, blackening everything that she tucks into the sock drawer, never tightening or loosening anything.)

"I'll tell you," I said, as though tossing down a few poker chips. "If you'll tell me *why*. Why you did not beat the crap out of me for all the bullshit I pulled. I mean, and then escaping down this porch you taught me how to build. Why, Dad?"

"I may just beat you, yet," he said, simmering a smile across his face. And then he crouched down, squatted really, his burly back against the now-shaky two-by-fours keeping us from falling overboard. "When I was ten," he said, "my dad left our house," he said. He had never spoken this before, even if I had figured it, sketched it roughly, siphoned it from tipsy Babica after she drank the dandelion wine. "He left our *family*. Left Babica. Left *Mati*. Me, my brothers and sisters. All eight of us."

I started to squat, too, but, losing balance, I fell on my legs and stayed there, letting them twist and hurt. Knowing not to move, like an animal playing dead. *"Dad,"* I said, giving like my last breath.

"Up until then," he said, "maybe four maybe six maybe eight nights a week my brother Damjan and me we would wake up— our room being closest to Mom and Dad's—and rush in. This was at maybe two or three in the morning. And pull my dad off her. Two kids. Can you imagine it? The other four slept through it. Used to the loud trains passing in the night... I don't know. He would have her wrapped in the sheets and blankets, wrapped up tight, his hand over her mouth. Her curlers still in. His hand over her mouth! But we could hear her," he said, and he could see her, now, he said, salmon-colored curlers choked by tightening sheets, she seeming the monster not the one on top of her, hammering into her his hundred little agonies. "Half the time half naked too, but we had no idea what he was doing, his pink rear in the air. *Vsemogočni Bog*. God."

And I heard, five miles away in the heart of the city, in the houses of the old Slovenian Ghetto, half of them hunkered-in by newly-arrived Mexicans, the winter wind whip in and slam a thousand closet doors closed, the jams busting off like buttons on a fat man's suit. Grandmothers woke without knowing why and kneeled before Guadalupe, lighting pink candles and praying for the repose of their dead and all who come here coiled with mortality.

The neighbor's garage door grinded open and I watched my father listen to the gears, wheels, pulleys squealing, watched him think how foolish they were for not taking ten minutes to oil the damn thing. Watched him check his weekend schedule for an open slot, for an hour during which he would come over there with a joke and a bag from the hardware store and fix their problems.

"He never laid a hand on us," he went on, his voice without saliva, rasping, every other word coming out with a high pitch. "But. But I wish he would have. *I* would have, I swear to you…"

"Hey. Who's there?" said the neighbor, Rick Wolfowitz, from where he stood, his small body buried in what appeared to be jogging wear—I'm still working to decode the occasional attire that proliferates out here, in the sprawl beyond the city. "All right. That's it. I'm calling the cops. Intruders!" he said, adding an artificial laugh that heed and hawed for a half a minute. I waited for my father to trade with him, to bow to custom and swap jokes, but the repayment never came.

"Shh. Shooting star tonight," I said, sounding as much like my father as I could. Proud of my proximity. After a moment Rick shuffled off, searching the heavenly bodies reluctantly as he went.

"Dad," I said, "I never touched my wife. I mean. I never laid hands on her like that."

He started to stand, his broad shoulders flexing, his whole body thickening in the cold. I pulled the collar of my secondhand parka—the blue one Sophia bought me for Christmas last year—up around my mouth. The mothball scent had given way to the Thieves oil she rubbed into everything filthy. I wondered whether it was still my turn. Took the coat off and offered it to him. My father is balding, has been since he adopted me, roughly. He rubbed my mess of hair and said, "You don't know what you got. You don't." He pinched the zipper and ripped the whole coat away from where it hung, lifeless, in my mourning arms. He tossed it up and over the railing and I stood tall, my legs asleep. We watched it descend, watched its hood catch on the clothesline hook, its zipper catch the kitchen light below and beam like a comet line, for a second, from silver to gold, before it collapsed into the window well.

"You were a sweet boy from the second you came out. The only one in the family who sleeps. And you always liked the nuzzles and the kisses like your mother. You always used to want the hugs. But I saw you don't now anymore," he said, giving me Babica's judicial eye, that impossible orb of merciful justice.

"I maybe never gave you enough. Affection," he said.

"Dad," I said. "*Oče.*"

"Don't," he commanded me, cuffing my wrist with his hand. "Listen. Maybe I never did. But listen. I don't want to hear how you never touched your wife like that. How you never laid your hands on her. I'm not interested too much in what you didn't do. But I've been wondering one thing for a long time. Do you ever? Touch her. Why am I going to die without ever having held a grandchild? Are you two…"

My arms stuck out like a poorly-clad scarecrow, and I swear I saw him look up, a terse search of the sky, as though he hoped a bird would blind me with dung for failing to give him descendants.

"I threw the salt shaker again. Fourth set of them we've gotten. Arbitrary. But it's a habit is what I mean. And this time I," my throat narrowed. "Shattered. The stained glass, I mean."

Earlier that day I'd combed through the weedy grass, trying to gather what I'd shattered, cutting my pointer finger on a chunk of it.

"Again?" he asked, his fingers finding just the right muscled areas of my hand and squeezing there where affection melded into punishment. Condemnation pursed his lips and then passed into something close to pleading as his eyes rolled up at the brilliant night.

"The stained glass was the first time," I contested.

"No kidding," he said. "There was only one window like that to break."

I dared not pull my hand away and in fact felt at home there, trapped there, in his hold. I stared at the reddening sections of my flesh, at his forceful thumb, the one carpel tunneled from pressing buttons at the brewery, and said, "When I was eighteen, just before I moved out, I'd come out here on this porch and want to jump off. Without a parachute mostly. This was the way I'd go. In the end I couldn't tell whether it'd kill me and I chickened out."

"Don't, don't hide. Not now. I'll buy you a new set of salt and pepper shakers," he said.

"Actually, the ones I threw, they're metal," I explained, "Steel, I think. Made to last."

"I'll work with you to put some stained glass back in that window," he said, "though *how we replace that kozmos-star Babica loved,* or what we'll put there in its place, God help us."

After a long pause he asked, "What you got in there now?"

"Nothing," I answered, ashamed that I could not at least putter out, "Plastic."

"And where is your *wife?* Where is Sophia? You left her in that cold house! And with the draft too?" he asked, letting go of my wrist after he had cut off the blood flow sufficiently. I looked at my hand, my limp and lifeless hand, at the hand that had done this to me. I searched for a scar, a mark left by his fingernails, his compression of compassion and punishment.

"*Sophia,*" he said again, and this time it came out as a question. "Your wife?" Her name. Her name.

"I. She's at a mutual friend's place tonight. I'll... call her in the morning."

"Call her tonight," he said. "Tell her to come here. I'll go into my room and keep quiet. I'll be asleep. If she comes, I'll be able to sleep," he said, speaking this last bit on behalf of my mother. He came at me with a tone familiar, one that had been restrained for many years: the primordial command. "You help me with the porch. Next summer. You promise. And I'll go down with you tomorrow and mend that window."

"Yes," was all I could conjure at first, until I managed "She's —I don't have her friend's number. She turned off her cell phone. Trust me, I tried," I watched the words to be sure they came out respectably, no tear in their chin-up eyes.

"Look," he said. "And you touch her," he said. "You take your hands and put them like this," he said, pulling my rubbery arms, my sleepy legs slackening. He put my hands around his shoulders until my chest was against his, my stomach concave against his convex. I smelled. I knew. Skins of sweat had been smothering my body and shedding ever since he'd said her name. He smelled as he always had—a faint tinge of grease and an undying aftermath of chamomile, which by some mystery were now part of his constitution, as real as the black follicles that looked now wolfish, now feline in the neighbor's flickering security light. He pried my snarly hair away from my forehead until he found my forceps wound that looked like a knotted X, and he pressed them there, his lips, his gristly chin against the outer lids of my closed eye, keeping the moistening that started to run, keeping it inside.

I knew I could make no return. God.

His finger caught on the collar of my coat and directed me down the stairs, following me a pace apart, coaxing me toward the garden with barely a nudge.

He darted at the little discarded nails of horseradish that had scattered in patterned chaos around the unburning bush. Like a famished rooster finally given feed, he pecked down and picked them up. Dropping them into my still-numbed hand he studied the pieces, all nonchalance. As I stood there startled, wavering, holding out the horseradish, my nose knowing the first pangs of its sweet reek, I watched him arrange the nails into the same cruciform that starred the stained glass window.

"We'll use this," he said matter of fact, obviously stating the obvious. "You broke the lead and the glass, right, I'm sure?" he asked, and I nodded. "Look, here. These are like the lead, when you line them up, they can run through the molded glass."

Vsemogočni Bog the sky's falling. Stars are born from the earth. *Vsemogočni Bog.*

"Let's get on over there now. I'll get the soldering iron. I'll get some old beer bottles and the shards of that vase of Babica's from the old country. Now she's dead she can't protest. It's been sitting useless in a closet for decades anyhow. I'll drive. You look like a drunk though you're a sober little s.o.b. tonight, son, you are aren't you?"

He waited for me to slump toward the car. He stood there. Loosed his glasses from his breast pocket, the thick plastic pair twenty-years-old. Licked each lens with a short dab and stretched out his T-shirt to wipe them clean. Then, as I slumped toward the car and creaked opened the door and negotiated my limbs inside, he, turning late, faced me straight on one last time, as though in disbelief. I twisted around. Light and warmth, reflected from God knows where, shone through his glasses like the noon sun. Its embers reflected blithely off of my father's lenses, one of which I had shattered, or he had, with the hug. He hung out his tongue, spat a chunk of glass out and closed his clear-lensed eye. Maybe he wasn't ready to see me whole. Maybe he knew I wasn't ready to see him see me. The divided lens glistened like the stained glass of a Gothic church and at it I stared adoringly, unsure what the eye on the other side could make out, exactly.

He ducked into the house in haste, brought out bags well-fed with shattered glass, nose of a soldering iron sticking out, horse-radish nails still faintly burning, burning faintly through the cheap plastic.

We drove down the lifeless, lightless streets, our burning

bodies shivering through the car's frugal heat, and as I opened my mouth to speak words of closure my stomach tensed, still hurting from his earlier affection. I remained silent.

Dad dodged a red-light runner without ceremony, did not swear or look back though it *thumped* us in the rear, and soon I heard his heavy frame collapse in the seat to the same sound it made when he descended, beat at the day's end, onto his marriage bed. Then came a sounding, either a sob or a sober laugh, muffled by his fisted right hand.

"You're a shit, you know that," he said. And then, gripping the steering wheel, "Love you."

I asked to be purged entirely of the words I would have uttered, whatever they would have been, as spoken they would have been a sacrilege on this night, on this night, on this silencing, shooting, starred night.

Work of
Human Hands

And by came an Angel who had a bright key,
And he opened the coffins & set them all free;
Then down a green plain, leaping, laughing they run,
And wash in a river and shine in the Sun.

Then naked & white, all their bags left behind,
They rise upon clouds, and sport in the wind.
And the Angel told Tom, if he'd be a good boy,
He'd have God for his father & never want joy.

And so Tom awoke; and we rose in the dark
And got with our bags & our brushes to work.
Though the morning was cold, Tom was happy & warm;
So if all do their duty, they need not fear harm.
—William Blake, "The Chimney Sweeper"

TWO WEEKS INTO private logic lessons and Father knew the scrawny kid would concede. The boy recited syllogisms with submission. The priest watched his roseate lips, pleased by their slightly-chapped curves. Never kissed. Rudy rewrote the *ad hominem* fallacy, copied what the priest had chalked on the board. Father waited until he finished. While Rudy pressed hard to form the last period, he smoothed his slim fingers down the boy's back pockets. He could not resist the never-kissed. Innocence always a lure.

"Father," said the boy. "Father."

For thirty seconds the priest feigned innocence.

"Did you take a piece of chalk without asking?"

Father let his fingers fall lower. Gravity. His touch lifted bumps from the boy's flesh, one hundred little pins poking out from within.

"Shhh. Peace. There's nothing to hide."

"Father, you can't—"

"Remember what I told you. You need to be good for your mother. She's having a hard time right now."

"Fa—"

The priest detected that confused desperation, the kind that whispered *I like this* but pretended to protest. He bent his neck in an arc that hurt. Curved like a swan, he breathed on the boy's neck, inhaling the skin's smell of cinnamon. Smiling. The priest preferred to keep his own clothes on. Classmates at Casimir Pulaski High School had called his dad "Bear," and he had inherited the hideous asymmetrical patches of fur that only came back thicker when he shaved them clean. In his vain twenties, when he drove down to the Chicago nightclub, Father spent Fridays lathering and scraping, sculpting himself smooth. Now he clothed himself in confidence.

Father wormed his fingers to the front, clamping the squirming kid with his legs. The priest grasped and found only air. Gripping one more time, he held something flimsy that wouldn't bait a baby—and heard the sound a mouse makes in a live trap.

The priest jerked his hand out, spun the boy around as he pushed him an arm's length away. Rearranging the little letdown's clothes, Father took great care to tuck in the shirt front, smooth the wrinkles away. Rushed blood retreated.

"It's okay, it's okay. You did better last time. You'll do better next time. Have a seat, now."

He returned to chalkboard and wrote out the next logical fallacy—*argumentum ad verecundiam*.

Arundhati's son had been flailing. Failing. After two weeks of waking at four a.m., pacing out her worries proved to be impotent. She called the parish office. Arundhati snorted when they promised her name at the base of the baptismal font. The check that paid for it came from her dead husband's life insurance. Blood money. When she saw ARUNDHATI ALIMON it looked like a brand name, gilded on a garish plaque that competed with the font for the onlooker's attention. She took a quick pull of the cool church air and let the frankincense collect her nerves. Her husband's death had made her wealthy beyond the brackets by which she had learned to measure money. She no longer sewed clothes in need of mending. She donated them to the poor of the parish through roundabout means that erased her entirely. And their son—who had his father's handsome face but not his father's hardboiled heart—was draining her mind. Clumsy. Flailing. Failing.

Someone at St. Rita's would know what to do. Listening to the low ring, she was prepared even to remind them of her most recent donations. A new roof. A new heater. Restoration of the stained glass. Arundhati waited on hold, reading her mother's naan recipe, searching it like the Scriptures for something concealed. Palm-muffled words piqued her attention. She strained to hear what the secretary was saying. The hand loosened and no longer garbled. "So sad, so, so sad. God takes the best ones for Himself."

Then Father's voice, especially boyish today, soothed.

"So good to hear from you, Mrs. Alimon. I was just thinking of you this past Saturday. We had a run of baptisms—all blessed by your open-handedness. That font really is *exquisite.* Now that it's here, the parish would be so bare without it."

The engraved name. She would start there. "Is there any way you can have the plaque removed, Father?"

The priest held his line. Public recognition was common practice. She was not being singled out. There was such a thing as false humility. He said this last playfully, almost in mockery. She took such things seriously.

Arundhati drew red herrings, objections like oil-slicked birds. The more she avoided the trouble with her son, the more a violent hue colored the conversation. When words came out she didn't know what they meant. She wasn't one to fight directly. Face-to-face felt like fencing without training, and it sapped her will quickly. Though they weren't head on, she could see him, jerking up, inching to the edge of the chair where, before she called, he'd been lost in the pleasantries of prayer. The recliner in his office tipped all the way back. Perched at the edge now, his mild annoyance petered into indifference. An oblong yawn.

Tired, too, envisioning the throbbing Adam's apple that dominated his homilies, she let the plea slip.

"Let's just let—I'm sorry. There *is* one thing you could do for me though, Father."

And she told him about her son.

"Rudy. He's always collapsing, breaking down at every little thing that goes wrong. He needs a good male influence in his life... I don't know. All our family's two states away. If you could, if you could just teach him something, anything really, and then let it turn into an outing once in a while. Get him to throw a ball around, maybe. My husband—he never... Rudy doesn't even know how to catch a ball, and he's so—sedentary. Sitting there in his room half the time since his father fell."

Still she could see him suspended in midair, falling from the massive stadium dome. The crowd would be covered. The games would go on in winter.

Because the boy knew the catechism decently and was already reading *The God of Surprises* for eighth grade religion at St. Rita's, they decided that he could try sessions in logic. These little lessons would, they agreed, be a pretext for the priest to teach him how to be a man.

When she found the stained underwear clumped in a pocket of Rudy's favorite pants, she forced from her son what Father had done. To hell with anesthetics. She pried, reaching with ruthless questions until she loosened the septic molars of his mind. Only after his contorted face stayed crimson a long while did she stop and make him lay across her lap like a baby.

She cut through the circumference of sanity, did curious things and did not find them strange.

Her thoughts went still stranger. Her dreams. In one the priest placed her son at a shrine to Our Lady. Except that Kali replaced Mary. The blue goddess, familiar from her Indian childhood, seized the priest and then swallowed him. Belching, Kali smiled before she stretched out four hands, fondling Rudy with all of them.

Evenings Arundhati could not be still, not with what she knew now. She brought in a babysitter.

Rudy retreated. It was embarrassing, old as he was, needing a nanny. From behind his bedroom door he mumbled this.

Immediately Arundhati swapped the sixteen-year-old for a college student. Less humbling for him. She increased wages and frequency after a week. Twenty dollars an hour. Mondays and Tuesdays and Wednesdays and Fridays.

"I don't know when I'll be back, exactly. You can just do what you need to do to keep up your studies. He'll be in his room, all you *really* need to do is sit next to the phone and walk upstairs every fifteen minutes to be sure he's alright. Try, I know it's hard, to get him outside. Even into the living room."

Resurrect him, can't you? What am I paying you for? Get him into the land of the living.

She circled the priest's rectory, studying his silhouette—now nearer, now disappeared—through the yellowed drape. For hours at a time she wound and unwound around the parish parking lot, then picked at his lawn until she knew every blade of grass by name. Feckless whoever mowed this place. She crawled in crooked spirals across the green, mimicking the punishment God should give the priest. Nebuchadnezzar on all fours. But the priest was the paragon of normal. If some nights he was unseen by the time she arrived, mainly he remained in the same place. Rocking in a chair doing God knows. Unchanging. Never looking out. Not even when she moaned under the weight. Nebuchadnezzar. Balaam's ass.

She did not want her friends to lose their faith, though they were disturbed by her sudden distance. She did not want the parish to peter out. Father must stay the same for them. All day long Arundhati swore to Jesus Christ, slurred indecipherable things. If He could comprehend them, she couldn't. If she knew Him before, now she didn't.

Sick tick. That's what another priest had named the grope, in the confessional, when she drove two hours to a different diocese, after the Chancery sent a form letter... *but we know that even unsubstantiated allegations can confuse and even be a source of scandal for the faithful...* She professed not her own sins, but Father's. "Not a sin, per se," said the foreign priest. "More like a *sick tick.*" Those did not seem like the right words, but she had not slept for months. She kept her knuckle over her mouth, kneading her gums. *Sick tick.*

She still went to Mass, her rare brown skin a beam in his eye. One Sunday the priest delivered a long homily. *If your right hand causes you to stumble, cut it off,* Jesus said. She could not resist a staring contest. She fixed on his hands which clutched there on the ambo. Crutches that needed to be cut. Father went off script. We should not take these words literally.

Arundhati walked out after communion. She ignored the DO NOT TRESPASS! and DOGS!!! signs that protruded above the picket fence and picked a lily from the priest's lawn. He owned no canines and was owed no property. At home she found her son outside, swaying from a rope he'd tied around an oak's thick thumb. She spied on him from behind hydrangeas, the flowers camouflaging her pink and purple sari. When the pendulum swings ceased and he leapt down grinning, she emerged and gave him the flower. Rudy dried and flattened flora into a big black book with a golden border. He knew their secret names.

"*Lilium,*" he said, laughing a little. Rudy stuck his nose in as she heard the buzz. He let it fall and his arms made mad swings after the bee until the thing fell to the earth. He laughed still more loudly, the way her father had at feasts, throwing his head back in infectious abandon.

My God, he's intact. She laughed, corrected herself. Laughed.

Rudy pinched the fuzzy body between the tip of his sole and the chalk-covered sidewalk, doing the same with his other foot before he handed back the flower and darted to the rope.

Arundhati filled the blue vase with cool water. The lily was too long, but she shrugged off the awful asymmetry.

She studied Rudy from within, hidden by the way the sunlight hit the window. Every few minutes he would leap from the rope and whack his temple with the butt of his palm, joshing or mad in the sun. On the stove, on low, the rogan josh simmered. When she lifted the lid the chilies stung her sinuses and she sneezed.

Then her nose swelled with spores of decade-old dust as she flipped through a phone book until she found it—the taped, almost faded number of a woman named Hazel who used to come to their parish until, the woman had told her, *I just can't take the double-vision, you know,* and winked. But the wink was more of a wince. Pressing her forehead against the freezer door, Arundhati dialed the barely legible number, forming fists and pinching her eyes shut, sure this was a dead end.

"Hello," a voice said, and at once she could see the uplift that always lifted Hazel's lips, mouth set apart from the strain that reigned over the rest of her face.

But she could not bring herself to tell. Instead she asked whether the woman knew any good priests, her question complicated by a wink. "He's always crumpling into a little ball," she said, "dying over every 'i' that doesn't have a dot." Outside, the arc of Rudy's swinging widened into a smile. "He needs someone who'll show him how to be a man, sitting there in his room all the time since his father died. And I really need the best you can recommend—but my expectations are low. Someone to throw back and forth a ball. But there's something else…"

Hazel nodded by saying *hmnh hmnuhm* every few seconds and her voice, which, though scratchy and slow, ended as though ascending with ease a high and rising road, said, "I know what happened. I can hear what happened. It's all over the way you sound, Ar." And her voice suddenly descended, like a loose car on a fast-spinning Ferris wheel, "Call Father Sun."

Father Sun, she said, was an old Chinese priest who still prayed in the old rite, but don't worry he would not speak Latin to her poor son, the one she remembered visiting in the hospital at birth, bringing him a stuffed porcupine that her own boy had played with as a baby.

"I'll be frank with you," Hazel said, "he's really sick with some unnamed illness that wracked him with all these aches. A friend told me he's hooked on painpills. Someone else said he's a high-functioning alcoholic. But I've never smelled more than a cough drop on his breath, and he's the holiest man I know. Every month I come back that way for spiritual direction. It may sound strange, but—"

"Nothing is strange."

"You're damn right there. Right. Here's the thing, though. Father Sun won't give you the run around about *we're all fallen* or the sympathetic shoulder pat or the same old B.S. about not all priests are like that."

The day of their meeting with Father Sun, Arundhati received a call from the secretary of Quietus Assisted Living. Father was not feeling well, but he insisted upon hosting them still. He apologized in advance, the secretary said, for the drool that fell from his lips each time he opened his mouth. On the way, the boy's mother fed him the same pablum she refused to ingest—about not all priests are like that. Ever since *it* happened she had let him either stay home or slink in the vestibule during Mass, and every time he accompanied her Rudy inched from the narthex back to the basement stairs, wrapped himself in the shadows there, where he waited for the end, waited for her to give him communion from an old golden pyx set aside for the sick. On the cover of the pyx a painstakingly-engraved Pelican fed its young from its own flesh. She could not look the bird in the eye.

As they opened the doors of Quietus his mother, eyes still full of midday light, nearly knocked over a famous once-journalist who had investigated and exposed the affairs of a famous once-president. At something like eighty-years-old he still had a baby face, and she could see that he was searching her for recognition. Arundhati gave him a low dose.

An old man with a small, almost shrunken head rushed toward them in a wheelchair. His face was dimpled and flushed like a ripe apple. He rolled across the faux-marble floor with a speed that made the wisps of his hair prick upward atop his mostly bald head. She took a step back and then, blushing, a step closer to him, extending her hand until, as he neared, his cassock caught in the wheel. She bent at her bad knee and worked it out, alternating between light tugs and yanks, pretending not to see the bib that he wore, assuring him with averted eyes that she did not see the pools of drool gathered there.

The priest could not speak. He put his fingers to his throat and made a flutter with his hands, tipping his head twice for them to follow him. Sun led them to his room, where he lit what looked like a cigarette from a votive candle. She recognized the dried eucalyptus leaf at once, as her father had chain smoked them well into his seventies. He handed it to her. First wheeling to the door and shoving it shut, Fr. Sun then flung the chair to the room's other end, throwing back a sapphire drape and punching the window open. He gestured for her to blow the smoke out. Then, giving Rudy a pained smile, he clamped the wheel brakes down and whispered "Sit down," pointing to two hard-backed chairs carved of beautiful oak. The room was emptied even of the obligatory TV that should have looked down from the upper corner opposite the bed. Under a handkerchief, four books slept against one another like siblings. *Summa Theologiae. Divine Office. The Long Loneliness. The Heresy of Formlessness.*

Arundhati breathed the smoke in, letting it cleanse her lungs like incense, blowing it out the window the way she had in high school, in India. She and her sister shared cigarettes on the second floor, when they were sure their parents were what they called "anchored"—too tired to rise from bed and reprimand.

Letting an old hoarse smile take form on his face, Father Sun reached his right hand out to the boy, who had been slinking behind his mother and now, forming hand puppets, produced little monsters on walls covered in a kind of sweet melancholic gloom. The priest pulled out a pair of cheap glasses with too-big rims, ovals that magnified his sad eyes. With his pointer and thumb he peeled back the lids until, seeing the creatures the boy produced, seeing them circle one another in mock battle, the priest let his neck slack until his head fell low, like a wounded swan. The boy, his hand fight finished, still stared at the wall, letting the priest's suspended hand shake mournfully in the empty air until his mother, aside to the priest said, "Unbelievable he's still doing this at near thirteen," and then, folding her arms, turned to Rudy and yelled through shut teeth, each word cut short before it could eke into existence, "Come. Out. Of. The. Shadows. Shake."

The priest's grip was so firm even the mother squirmed, sure that her boy would break.

"What is your name, son, young man?" he mouthed, spending whatever breath he could muster to give the words sound.

"Rudolph," said the boy, and for once no one said *"Like the reindeer?"*

"This is your mother. Do you know how she loves?"

Rudy nodded.

"One of my brothers has stolen something from you. Do you want me to get it back?"

"Fucking kill him. Three times," Rudy said.

Arundhati formed a fist, covered her mouth.

"Do you want me to?" Father Sun tilted his head like a fascinated child.

"Don't touch him. Don't touch me. No one touch anyone ever again. Don't talk to me about it. You tell me it'll pass, I'll roll you down the hallway."

"Rudy."

Then something happened. Father Sun's head fell again. His neck, noticeably long, looked choked.

When he woke a few breaths later he backed away from Rudy but kept his gaze fixed on the faint wrinkles that curved down around the boy's pale lips.

"Have you ever gone to the amusement park?" he managed, the question just audible to Rudy's perked ears.

Rudy shook his head no.

"We'll go sometime, just before it closes, in the evening, in the dark. The three of us. My treat," he said, and the boy's mother pressed her fist over her mouth, as the priest seemed to miraculously regain his voice. "You'll see all the bodies swirling around in saucers that spin and coasters that rise and fall faster than empires do in God's very way of weighing time. And then you'll take a ticket and wait in line. Look at the thing, whirling, wheeled around forever, lit up with a thousand bulbs. When you come down you'll look at their faces. The people waiting in line. You won't like what you see. There's many hungry people there," and here a *tsk* came as he nearly choked, "keep riding. Never get sick of it. Never getting sick."

But, though he cleared his throat three times, and wheeled into the little bathroom to gargle, Sun's voice would not return. Rudy's mother watched each twitch around her son's eyes as he listened to this odd Father, watched his eyebrows elevate at *never getting sick*—and the whole story came out awful. Hazel, too, had lost it, taking her here.

Father Sun reached out and retrieved the cigarette, which had petered out into a butt between her fingers, forgotten. He tottered toward a chest of drawers and deposited the pinched thing into the top one. Then again he dusked from consciousness.

Arundhati reached for Rudy. He reached for the door but slipped.

As he nursed his cramped leg, Father Sun woke. Rising gingerly, he leaned toward Rudy, who jolted over and caught the falling priest and propped him against the drawers. Balancing his body with his good arm, Father searched the bureau somewhat frantically until, nodding, he heaved out an old black book whose edges were light red like the priest's face. Father Sun's eyes flitted fiercely across the pages. His shoulders scrunched and his neck shot out as he searched. Peering into a prayer at the very end, he nodded again and mouthed the words, ignoring the absence of sound, and in the naked room his rasps came out loud. He pressed his hands against the boy's head, rubbing in the water he had sprinkled there, holding his hands against Rudy's temples until the trembling in his hands ceased, then until the boy stopped shaking.

At the end he asked Rudy to please wait just outside the door.

"Please. You must tell the right person. Tell the bishop," he mouthed to the boy's mother, scrounging all of his strength—as a mother does with a scouring pad after all the children are in bed and the pans remain filthy—to get the words out. "If the bishop does nothing go higher, and higher, until you reach the Pope himself. And tell me," he whispered, the sound brittle and broken. "If you want me to say anything for you. Anything. I will at once so long as God grants me life. Until then," he said, folding his hands and holding them high.

Arundhati mouthed *thank you*, put her hand on his shoulder. He placed an unlit eucalyptus leaf in her palm. She noticed almost no one as she shot down the hallway, searching for Rudy. She nearly knocked over a nurse's aide, bumped into a tray of juice. The claret water spilled everywhere and she fled Quietus like a fugitive.

Rudy was waiting in the back seat, nodding off. He started snoring halfway home, and she did not wake him until dusk.

Over the next three days she worried through three packs of cigarettes and one pair of shoes, ruined by a stray corkscrew on the rectory lawn. The metal didn't puncture her skin.

Arundhati did not care if an officer came. If one did, she decided, it would be a sign and she would tell all. Neither neighbor nor policeman asked her why she was acting suspicious. Sometimes a few people—and always the same ones—watched her through their own drawn shades. Lights would go out when they saw her see them move. Their fixed eyes remained. No officers ever came.

She could not tell the bishop. He was the priest's good friend. A dead end. She would scare the sick ticker out herself. Every morning at six she showed up for daily Mass. She kept her hands to herself, especially during the sign of peace, and as they exited the narthex on Sundays Arundhati glared at the garmented impersonator of Christ, laughed aloud at his charm. Once, during a baptism, when his hands cupped a naked baby, she punished him with a dropped jaw and a head shook from side to side, surreptitiously, until she snapped out of it and prayed *"Help!"* The parishioners punished her in return, a sea of condescension punctuated by a few sympathetic faces.

One day, after Rudy shoved a chair down the stairs, she dropped a can of deviled ham at his doorstep and rang the bell. Picked from a bag she had bought for the pantry. Like an adolescent playing a prank, she hid behind his pear tree, waited. She heard the screen door, bent from its hinges, screech. Her husband would have set it right. Father stood up straight, stayed leaning against the siding, awaiting a firing squad. He stood there considering the can, peering around the yard. Just as he turned to go back in she walked across his wet grass. Heavy steps brought her within feet of him. The priest pocketed his hands. A tic electrified his lips until he bit them still. Elbows bent, hands against her hips, she gave him silence.

Leaving, she looked back. When she did he moved toward her, arm outstretched, dropping the can and extending his empty hand. He looked like a lost boy who has mistaken a stranger for mother. Arundhati almost returned, but a gnat made her blink, and when she looked again he did not have any eyes. Only two holes holding two whirling voids. He fell and chalked a line around his dead body. But when she blinked again he said "I—"

After such knowledge, what forgiveness? His black shoes clacked on the stone path that took him home, and she was sickened by how well those shoes shined under even the low watt street lights. Still later, she heard him pounding boards across the windows' insides. The burglaries were bad that year.

Nails clattered even in her dreams that night, pinned Kali to a formless darkness. A lone soldier hammered them into Kali's flesh, fixing blue skin to the amorphous black until an eclipsed sun spun down to the earth, its sliver of light a scythe, and then it was evident that everywhere, in orderly lines that seemed never-ending, bodies were hammered to the formless waste. The scythe of sun grazed. Some bodies remained uncharred, others set fire and refused to burn. When the sliver of flame kissed Kali she groaned resistance, writhed and contorted and mocked the light. Hisses shot out from the goddess, as when ancient tree limbs buckle begrudgingly—defeated at last by the terrible heat. Snap.

Arundhati woke with a strained neck, sweaty hands, scared. 3:29. Wide-eyed, she went into Rudy's room and pressed her palms against his temples. She prayed. First memorized words, like the empty cars of a cargo train. By sunrise she meant what she was saying, like an overburdened caboose loaded with goods. Her sweaty hand laid against her son's forehead. She dialed Hazel. No answer.

The priest called and called, leaving short messages on the family phone. The machine still played her husband's voice. Father said the same thing every time. "I would like to talk to him. And you." The words grew shriller as winter came, breathing its enduring chill.

At last, on Christmas Eve, he gave them silence.

By Christmas evening Father was beyond wearied. Four Masses in less than a day. At the parties he botched every joke, took too many pulls from the holiday punch, dispensing no cheer to parishioners. Evelyn Hacker, church elder, pulled him into a side room and gave him a grand inquisition. Her clairvoyant eyes narrowed when he cracked a signature joke. "Something is not right," she said to him, "Father, I know you priests can't confide in us, but I'm here. I'm here."

Tipsy from her cranberry punch, the taste of cinnamon still on his tongue, the priest slumped over to the church. At the end of the aisle his knees went slack. Slouched at the edge of the Nativity. In the dark he reached out to cradle the baby. He rocked and crooned Christ to sleep, cooing like a fool in the quiet. But then his hands betrayed him—*sick tick* or doubt, or the cool of the ceramic crèche. When he dropped the pallid porcelain Jesus, begging, as he did so, that the child punish him, the scratchy clang did not end with a bang. Only the hand cracked off and slid across the floor, and even the stump seemed to wave with elation. The baby smiled up at him, intact.

As the bedsprings protested against his tossing, he turned over the boy's eyes, the way they looked after Mass for all these months, shaded in the vestibule as though charred by hard coal. His consciousness choked like an overtaxed chimney sweep and he heard the boy speak in a voice soft and warm, *So if all do their duty they need not fear harm... and the Angel told Rudy to keep his mouth shut except tell God the Father that the priest touched his butt. And did else beyond telling and still more with many more.*

In the morning the priest felt as though he had tried to cross the Atlantic in a little fishing boat, but the buckling waves put up their fists and flung him back to the same spot he had started from. He set out again, a rower all alone, straddling the stern before it sank under his weight, succumbing to the silence of the sea as he swam to shore—a cluster of bobbers like red lesions wounding the water where the boat had been. Or... that was his last dream before a west wind whisked his silvering hair with its gray exhalations.

Awake, he skipped the shower and walked out the door. He would find the shears in the tool shack in the back of his dad's house, the one he and the neighborhood boys had built for Babica. When he and his brother Blaise were teenagers, his hands had cut Blaise down from the shed ceiling. Found him there on a whim. Never told their dad.

His mind would go back there whenever he did wrong, seizing that one good deed to cancel the bad ones.

Dim blue dusk the skylight let in, colored the hanging man's skin purple. No. *I am not here. This isn't happen*—

When Father was four his mother left him alone in the waiting room for a long time. She came back dabbing moist circles of mascara around her eyes. He had colored the skin of the skinny cosmopolitan ladies who looked at him longingly, hungrily, from the covers of magazines. *"They* don't have *kids,"* his mother had muttered, as though to herself. But he heard her. They all turned purple, the ladies without kids he had colored. Digging into her purse, whose innards he scattered across the green carpet, he had found a whole blue crayon. LAPIS LAZULI, the crayon read, though he could not decipher the meaning. He had ripped off the cover of COSMOCEPTION and folded it along four crease lines. The way he did with the towels at home. *Mommy's little helper.* Tucked her into his pocket and pulled her out sometimes at night. When he had unfolded her and set her against his pillow like an icon, little ejaculatory prayers came out. *Please!* He would lean over, dizzy somehow, mouth muffled against the bed edge. He did not know why. Why when he colored blue the woman's orange skin it had turned the color of his bruises. "He plays hard," his mother would say. "It's good for him. A boy should have a few bruises." He did not know why. Maybe there was a gloss on everything and it came undone when you rubbed it off, a gloss that felt slipperier than human skin and gave everything a glow. Bruises. The color of exhausted blood in the veins.

And how his brother had turned that color, too. Death. The color of choked blood. The dim blue dusk the skylight let in came as a kind of crayon that purpled his brother's blue flesh. His brother an uprooted turnip, hanging. Blued at the tip and the rest blanched. He heard a *spft* and *fehp* and felt Blaise's spit sprinkle his hands. *Not dead yet.*

One eye shut from a sudden ache that gripped half his head, he had spiraled and then turned at sharp angles around the shed, rifling through boxes, spilling mummified swans that had belonged to their mother and sometimes filled the center of the dinner table. Swans that broke at the neck as they hit the floor. *Who cares God who cares God you care?* A blade beneath where the swans had slept, wrapped in tissue paper. A rusted garden shears that remained stiff for two tries until, during the third, it snipped the rope, interrupted the pendulum swing. He stepped back, unable to break his brother's fall. The noose still snaked around his throat. His brother, the purple bleeding into a raw meat pink, picked up a swan neck and threw it against the shed wall. Their sad eyes met as the neck ricocheted against the wall but would not break. Without expression—lips neither pursed like a dog's when yanked by a leash nor flared into a horse's wizened smile nor twisted like a happy horror clown. Flat line across his mouth, cut down, Blaise coughed, undid the noose, asked with voice steeped in vinegar, "Why, and how'd you know?"

"I don't know." He reached out and touching the head of the empty noose whose fibers still curved into a circle though cut. "I didn't know. God. I was just coming back from a run. Thought I heard an animal in the shed. Blaise!"

But Blaise quit the shed, and he disappeared for a week, returning like a limp Lazarus just when their folks had given him up for dead.

The good son. He would play the good son. Last time Father went home Dad had hinted that the porch needed a lift—something he "hadn't gotten around to yet." A perfect excuse. A belated Christmas present. *"You need help, dad? You do. The porch, look at it, it's about to keel over. Gimme the keys to the shed and, I insist, you just relax and I'll—"*

While Dad boiled blood sausage, cooked kraut for a long lunch, he would disappear into the shed, find those old shears. Surely at the wrist the sinews and bone would give under the blade. Greasy rags there, plenty of cloth to tourniquet the blood. Hard to remove both hands by yourself. Impossible, maybe. No one else. One of his parishioners, a refugee from Nigeria, had his right hand cut off for theft. The priest had preached hard on the injustice of it all. But his parishioner had stolen only food.

When they released him from surgery or jail cell or asylum, he would find a way to say one last Mass at St. Rita's, elevate the host with the nubs, not even the nubs but the thorny stitches that stuck out like stick fingers from a child's first drawing.

Even this would fail. Fool. Eclipsing the sun with an inflated widow's mite.

Nothing would show what he had to say straight to the boys, the men, the mothers and fathers, the millions of others his crimes would arrest.

Old Blood

We have retreated inward to our minds
Too much, have made rooms there with all doors closed,
All windows shuttered.
There we sit and mope
The myth away.
                    —Elizabeth Jennings, "In This Time"

AT FIVE MINUTES PAST TWO a waif in gray pinstripe pants, a narrow black tie, and a pomaded crew cut shook his undersized umbrella gently, surreptitiously, and ducked in from the whetted ash of the Milwaukee afternoon. His flesh was pigeon-gray. Inside, eyes pinging between golden globes of dangling light that hung over one hundred ovular tables, he handed his umbrella to a stout cashier with sad eyes and a floating smile that did not seem part of her face. She hesitated, breathing in and turning still redder than the rosacea already made her, holding the metallic ribs covered in plastic the way a child holds a dead bird, perched there on the front porch, preoccupied with the flightless thing and so unwilling to reach out and ring the bell.

Enough.

The metal and plastic fell and clanked as with one hand she held the cash register closed, her shaking other searching for her phone. Dirt already under the just-cut fingernails. The waif's scrawny hands, feigning elegance with gray gloves so soft, clamped around her wrist. Look up. His eyes calm, almost kindly, as her leg shook. "Get yourself something nice, somewhere," he managed to say without moving his jaw, prying open her clench until she parted it and he placed there a ten dollar bill, mouth-shut until he gave her a reassuring smile, betraying a hole where an incisor once was, nodding toward the door of the university cafeteria. Then the turnstile spun and erased her into the drear. A janitor who sat next to her on the same 22 line—who had almost stayed home on account of the gross greenish mucus that lined her eight-year-old's eye—dropped the mop mid-ring and watched a chalky, inky splash dirty the floor she just had finished cleaning. "God help me, Jesus! Girl! Hold up!" she shouted, leering sideways at the ghost of a man, giving a fierce, v-shaped brow and forgetting her bum ankle as she shot after the cashier and also escaped. Her son. She'd nearly kept him home, but his attendance was awful and the scholarship that staid him at St. Jude's... Her son. She slouched towards him. She did not look back.

A student, bent over to breathe in the dark chocolate heat of her double mocha, lipstick moistening and coloring the pale cup purple, looked up from a text message that said LOL HELL YES! and saw the ghost of the man's heart slip through his teeth as he filled her and sixteen other bodies with soft point bullets.

No one in the whole cafeteria recognized him, though most did manage to get a good glimpse of his resigned eyes, and the itching lower lip reined in by a bite. He did not say a word before, during, or after he riddled seventeen bodies dead.

Countless shots. Someone would count them. Part of the ritual. A tally. Pick up the pieces put them in a pot and cook some sense out of it all.

He watched them fall the way his grandpa, who had worked the cornfields for fifty years, watched stalks collapse, satisfied to see them arch toward the earth under gravity's ache. As if what he did to them would have happened regardless, not on account of his gun but because of some larger circuitry of causality that he brought to inevitable and enlightened completion. He did not run when the police came. His tongue never touched the muzzle of the pistol, tasted neither the metallic barrel nor the small columns of lead with which he had reduced the total world population of debtors. As sure of his purpose as he was a surefire. Impeccable aim.

The shooter spared journalists everywhere the familiar ritual of rifling through internet scrawlings and interviews with friends to find the true motive. "Saving them lives of misery," the police report quoted the killer. "I'd rather be in prison anyhow," he went on, "than keep living under the long arm of the bank. Con game. College. Conspiracy."

In the hidden back alleys or basement furnaces or over-whelmed sewers of his chemical synapses? No despair there. No record of therapy or of psychotropics; he was not known to have been an inpatient or an outpatient. Bosses bespoke his signature calm, an assumed asset that now seemed a lie.

The man, Michael Watt, had taken the Greyhound to Char-lotte a year earlier to work in internet technology for Bank of America. He had remained there, with punctual punch-ins, "a real hard worker, if not the best collaborator, but many from IT aren't," his supervisor said, leaking nothing when the frog-throated reporter rattled him, asking if it was true that they fired Watt for asking too many questions about privacy and piracy and the easy-to-puncture protections coding customer data. Watt had studied computer science and philosophy at Mar-quette. His unpaid student loans amounted to eleven thousand, ten percent of the debt he had acquired when he had walked across the stage at commencement. (He had not walked across the stage at commencement. "They spoke his name through the microphone," his ethics professor said. "I gave him a little nudge with my eyebrows, a little nod. He just held onto that seat. Knees in. Legs angled out.")

Ex-girlfriends named him a gentleman, cited his humor and roses. His creditors claimed no qualms—no missing monies. No payments delayed. His case made no sense. Given his salary, several more years at his current rate of repayment and the bright blue bills that both blew up on his screen and appeared, nonluminous and redundant in the mail, would have ceased completely.

Millions and millions of eyes scrutinized the Marquette alumnus, half-listening to the reporters, who bantered from the crime scene to the newsroom and back, the camera lights like luminous fingernails scratching their heads and faces as they tried to say what was right.

Millions of others turned off devices, swapped sites, switched channels, replacing the clean-cut killer (*my son's age… my brother has that shirt… looks like my grandson… who're his parents?… that day I almost did it*), surging whatever was not him into the swelling images burning their minds. Sucking in anything else at all and so drowning out the shooting. Flushing him out in the whirling toilets of their brains. But the stench remained, the mucky waste making its way back up clogged pipes and filling the noses of their souls. Choke. Click away.

* * *

Laying across her yellow couch, a woman looked around her own home as if it were a hotel. Each time she flexed her leg or turned from side to back, the leather let off the sound of an untouchable, well-fed cat savoring a hand-rolled treat. Cities and cities away from the Milwaukee gray that glowed from her screen, she shook a plastic chute colored the warning orange of traffic lights. Two pills instead of one fell into her palm, and she stuck these little medicinal bullets between her fore and her middle fingers for play. Forming her hand into a faux gun, she feigned a trigger against her temple before she stuck the make-believe muzzle into her mouth. Next she swallowed them and shook the remainder as though for good measure—to be sure more remained. The column, wrapped in warnings and side effects unreadable in the soft light, seemed to make a sucking sound, jealous of its contents. *Whooip.* Stuck. Half undone, drowsed under the mellow droning sound that emanated from the tuning forks and the high strung harps that sang in the hollows of her bones, she arrested an armful of strength and tossed the pill bottle at the screen. A few loosened and flew forth like black stars shooting against the milky gray screen.

Like a child at play she crawled across the floor. Scraped them from the carpet. In her palm the little things looked like untended eggs, harmless and helpless and in need of nurture. (This though in a small pinhole of her soul she knew they would care for her, comfort her, take her into their unknowing dark.) Without them she could no longer sleep. Not ever, but especially not tonight, as the young man who did what he did in the cafeteria—which also looked so familiar, looked even like the one at her new workplace, as though dining spaces were increasingly cut from the same mold, designed by the same mastermind and made in the same factory—was the one she had known through the internet; she had dated and even almost moved to Charlotte for him, for his letters, those long scrolls of tenderness that told her only about her. Never about him. After six months she stopped answering. Did not tell why.

Now, curled up against the West Coast, looking out on the ocean from the glass-walled condo her uncle had given her when, no longer able to go it alone, he surrendered to the nursing home, childless as he was and her godfather. (That supposedly meant something, him being her godfather, but she had never known exactly what, since neither of her parents believed in God.) She kept the lights out nearly always, trying to figure out how so many of her drapeless neighbors could live on display, seen by so many who stalked and walked and panhandled below (though she bit her lip at this, balked at her own vanity), waiting for the blinds she had ordered last week, upon arriving here. Her job—combing through spreadsheets of dental records for insurance companies—gave her the flexibility to move here from Texas and keep the same salary, the privilege of working from home, alone, all alone. All along. Except she could not do alone what she did now. Endure.

Quick. Crush the little pills into particles still smaller. Numerous as the sands of the sea and therefore split up into so many—powerless. Descendants. *He* had wanted children, even. One of the categories on the singles site. The first man she'd dated who didn't recycle some variant of the same: "How could I bring children into this world?" The killer, though, sent his older sister's children not only birthday cards but coloring book pages created by an algorithm he had made with his own hands. Michael. He had served as babysitter according to the algorithmic semi-randomness that ruled the busied lives of his childhood neighborhood, babysat the whole neighborhood's brood when young. All of this unburied from the plastic bins of a past so long shoved into the back corner of a garage, so long coated in mildew, kept beyond consequence under decades of dust. One of his former charges, then seven and now seventeen, spoke into the microphone, his skin just a touch lighter than the black foam. Watt did scold him once, scared him out of his mind and made him conscious of things he'd not yet known. The killer had cut short the kid's cavalier discharge of squirt gun water, insisting that if the police happened to cruise the street at the same time as he pulled the trigger they might not pause to parse between cold-blooded killer and childhood playthings. The shooter had said this. Stunned, the kid kept this newfound fear to himself and crunched underfoot the toy he'd nagged his parents for. Shoved the shards through a sewer grate. This was the only sign. Otherwise, under the spotlight, Watt's well-lit life contained no clue.

* * *

Watching it all from his wheelchair, unable to hear but squinting so as to follow the scrolling caption across the bottom of the television, a seventy-three-year-old leaned close to the screen and cleaned longstanding smudges with his wet, faded red handkerchief. Arrested, he watched. He who had shot and killed a village under orders, killed and shot them as they sat there eating, told himself while eliminating them that they'd be freer as ashes, sifted and slipping through the shaky hands of the American army and the ruthless fists of the Communists both. Cleaned the screen to see the scene more clearly. The shots of sprawled death sheared from his mind the woolen lies, stripped the sophisticated yarns that softened what he'd done. Barbed wire and bones and bullets. Babies too small to breathe without milk. (Say one were to survive, crawl out from the ash of a collapsed house, tomorrow, after the soldiers had passed on to the next mission. No more. No heartstrings tied to babies in war. Future enemies. Babies. No. No babies.)

Mothers' moans that melted the red-blooded moon. Last breaths of children but most made instantly quiet, little wheezings eerier in combat, the quiet crueler somehow. (Armchair watchers elsewhere, condemning but benefiting. Did what I did to keep the world safe. You don't know how good you got it. What he said to his draft-dodging brother the last time they talked.) Lapsing thoughts. Disappearing like the beers they drained that night. To keep from throttling their commander over the atrocity. What Henry had put in his veins thereafter, in Vietnam. Half the troops steeled and steady heroes, half coupling with the same mistress heroin. As old as Helen in Homer, who out of Egypt brought home a medicine that erased.

Lapsing thoughts. As though his head refused the blood the heart sent there. Unable to let both live and let live the truths that threatened to throb. Cutting off circulation until he was outside of himself, unconscious of all the dying thoughts that had hounded him, studying the man in the wheelchair like a portrait painter, gleaning the substance from the surface, thrilling at the way the watercolor eased the loneliness into pastel impressions, until he became a forgotten hero finally given his flying colors. Levity. But then the IV drip kinked and he sat up and again saw the blood on the TV. Almsgiving covers a multitude of sins. *I'll never earn enough alms to cover the graves I made.* Almost ceased his breathing until a loud and irritating ring roused him.

"Can you hear me, Unc?" she asked, stretching out on the couch that crooned like a petted cat, extending her hand to the artificial fireplace whose digital flames gave off heat, "I'm just calling to be sure you're okay. I've been worried you're lonely in that new place. I'm looking at tickets. You can pay to have someone assist you on the airplane. A kind of aid. You wouldn't need to travel alone. Just a thought. This place is... actually, a little big for me. And I'm not getting married anytime soon. Not to say never. Not that I'm complaining. But you'd"—she almost caught these last words and buried them in a cough, so stupid they sounded— "you'd be welcome here. We could find a home nurse. A nurse who comes into the home. I know you were worried, when you lived here, about outside. Not outside on the street but inside it's safe here."

She knew, shy as he was, hesitant at every turn, his silence meant *yes*. Still, bent forward as she waited, she scratched at the old sore that swelled at her knee, felt the old blood fall in caked crumbs to the floor. When she lifted her finger and found fresh crimson there, she said, "Unc, come on home."

Some Other Exit

SHE WALKED WITH CALCULATED CLICKS that made her feel weightless, her heels hardly touching the red carpet as she floated down the very long hallway of AIPOT Bank's seventeenth floor, and, having survived that claustrophobic bringer of heart palpitations—so different from the high ceiling, open-concept design of their house, and even the wide open community room of the nursing home where she taught Contrology classes—she peeked in through the cruciform window of the last office door on the left. Her husband sat there, still, giving the screen an attention so rapt she could not help but feel it as affection.

For the sixth night in a month the dinner alarm, wired through his consciousness with such permeation and precision that it until now had interrupted even the most elevated immersion in his work, failed. Now, with sixteen Excel sheets opened on the screen, he cut and pasted from them with staccato inhalations followed by satisfied sighs that anyone listening to could have reasonably registered as swoons. Tuesdays he always met her at the Calm and Collected Café, where of late they plied sushi-grade tuna fish and problems with their eldest, who had disappeared weeks before and now regularly called at two in the morning—as though his parents would be sleeping, as though the machine would catch his voice before his mother awoke and answered, as though she had not taken to dozing in an almost standing position, her body propped between a stool and the kitchen table, her efforts to release the reins of consciousness effective for twenty minute increments at most before her posture went perfect and she gripped the reins again, riding restlessness until the rising sun reached into the house. He'd called just to say "I'm alive" and hung up.

She'd told her husband about their Keith's pierced face, his new role as scowling neon singer of a band called CORIOLANUS. She'd seen the poster on the vestibule corkboard of a Cheap and Dear Market. He had asked her if she took it down. Married minds. Seeing it, she had torn it down and shredded it into the cigarette ashtray. Trashing it would make the trouble disappear, or at least disintegrate. He reeled back, when she told him, as though her tongue had stretched out and stung him. The wasabi made the tears easier to do.

Having dropped the other children at their Responsiveness Lessons—it was true that she had almost taken them to the Confidence Classes, before remembering that those came on Thursdays—she had hurried over to his office to repossess Richard from his job, where he'd been staying late since she told him about CORIOLANUS. She trusted him, yes. Yes, she trusted. But it wasn't unreasonable to be sure he was not at an unmentionable Somewhere Else.

She stared at her hunched husband, *noooowh* escaping her lips, the same sound that came when her mother passed, as if her husband was not working but was actually dead there, in the chair. She shook her head, a flit of hysterics electrocuting and then leaving her. She held her breath, cheeks ballooned by her son's defiance, but could not help laughing. His huff. So dramatic. Punch drunk around this time every night, sleeplessness having the same effect on her as the amphetamines they found in Keith's unkempt underwear drawer. She squinted at her reflection in the window, her phantom face. It seemed for a second translucent, and she could see it all: the chaos of her mind's chemicals chasing her will like a mob after a fleeing tyrant. *I am who I am,* she said, repeating the mantra of her Contrology instructor.

Her husband was not applying her advice regarding posture. She had tried to show him even just the pictures of her *Seven Days to a Straight Back* book, especially the centerfold poster that outspread into a sort of evolutionary pictography of the Better Back, starring a man who looked as neutral as the figures on airplane emergency manuals, the same man morphing from far-left hunched (velociraptor hands extending over the keyboard) to the far-right fixed, where he had no more curvature than a flagpole.

Bent over accounting sheets, Richard's hand scratched the gray-black curls above his ear every thirty seconds, celebrating the completion of each calculation as he tallied the day's transactions. Infallibly, the workday always ended in a growth that, after running his eyes up and down columns of numbers for nine or ten hours, drew a sigh from a place that seemed to transcend his stomach but always heaved heaviest there. His was the task of measuring the miniscule privations against the weight gained, of measuring how many inches the giant hand puppet of interest increased on the wall, lit up by the burgeoning wattage of AIPOT-advised portfolio investments, a figure that could only be found by setting against this impressive shadow the following: every cent the bank paid people to lend it money to lend out that same money to other people, so they could lend out to other people, who could therefore lend it out to other people, to lend out to other people, to lend to other people, to lend people out to lend.

In thirty years he had made only one (mentionable) error of calculation, about a week before on the day he turned fifty and could not be moved by a single classic rock song, no matter how many he put on the old record player of his youth, fifty years and a day by the time she found him at the bar near two thirty a.m., inserting more coins into the jukebox than it could possibly require, blinking out at her bit lips before he returned to the selections and entered the code for "(I Can't Get No) Satisfaction." No alcohol on his breath as she accepted his invitation to slow dance in the darkened corner of his favorite haunt, a place otherwise populated by Hell's Angels, vested in their priesthood's leather, burning skulls looking out on the couple who moved without conforming to the rhythm, less hurried than even a high school slow dance. And then she spotted another one—a neon pink flier tacked forcefully over fifty other competing pleads for the attention of those passing into the restrooms, a cartooned image of her son gripping a microphone and giving the finger under CORIOLANUS LIVE AT RAG-E-TIME, with special guest TITUS ANDRONICUS in cryptic font, the white space beneath the stage informing the onlooker that "THE BODY POLITIC BELIES US!" at which point her arms went slack and she could not continue even the slow rise and fall, left foot then right foot. Instead, she tiptoed to kiss Richard on the neck, beckoning him to their bedroom, keeping his gaze from their poster child.

When I'm watching my tv and a man comes on and tells me... It was true that they had taken him to a Rolling Stones concert when he was only twelve, but the evening had seemed so harmless, little different than the basketball games that they also frequented at the same stadium, the lead singer rather than the star player occupying most of the pixels of the colossal, four-sided screen. Magnification of everything. True it was three times the price, which had prompted Richard to recalibrate their budget, so that the cupboards were absent marshmallow pies for three weeks.

And besides, she thought now, shaking her head over Keith, surplus recompense continues to pay dividends. Her kept-in thoughts disobeyed, fled, fogged up the office window. Her watch said that the children's Responsiveness Lessons would end in fifteen minutes, and as it took ten just to walk down the hall, she would be late.

As though his rapt forgetting was contagious, she watched him watching, because that was all he was doing now, watching a video of clearly their son though pierced and (it seemed) tattooed around (even) the eyes, her husband (actually) nodding to the drum which was more automatic weapon than instrument, his melodic "My rage is gone, and I am struck with sorrow," a counterpoint to the crescendo of cymbals and the synthetic, scratchy screeches of the guitars—conquering more than accompanying them.

He knew even more than she did, maybe, then.

She could not bring herself to rap at the cruciform window, but it was true she was bothered that he had not noticed her there, had not felt her familiar eyes upon the neck hairs which she had grown not to notice. Back to an algorithmic rhythm of clicks by which he balanced the Excel sheets, which is to say that not a single transaction escaped or exceeded the Master Sheet, after which he sat back in a rare rest that she had not seen in decades, the rests he embodied at home always splayed in catlike and catatonic stretches across the great eucalyptus-colored couch, or the bored ghostings with which he entertained things important to his children, his fingers moving the SORRY pieces almost apologetically, although a faint watt of delight flashed from his eyes like a hotel vacancy sign when they played Monopoly.

Finally she tapped, five minutes before the instructor would dismiss their children from Responsiveness.

"Sweetie, I need you to get the kids from lessons." She spoke with caution as he opened the door, cutting off his apologies with "You're—honey. I love you hon. I need you to pick up the children now, yes, you'll be late. They have a lady who stays there afterward just in case. It isn't written anywhere, but when I've been even five minutes after I give her a ten, so maybe a twenty would be right."

"Are you alright?—of course you're not," he asked and answered.

"I'm going to get him," she said.

"Going where? To get him where are you going to get him?"

Her averted eyes escaped the avidness of his ocular attention, finding a calendar affixed to his cubicle, affirming that today agreed with one of the barroom flier's tour dates, which she had clearly failed to willfully forget. *That* was what had set her stray thoughts in catlike curls around her lost son, *not* her husband's internet stalking of the flesh of their flesh.

"CORIOLANUS is putting on a show in the basement of the AIPOT campus housing. The part they've turned into dormitory housing. Remember that article from last Sunday's paper? He'll be down there. I have to see him, let him see me. At least." All of this said with the elevated shoulders of an Atlas as though indifferent to the pains of his carried weight, but at the edge of the straight line of his lips you see the recalcitrant grimace going nowhere.

"*I'll* stay. I'll go," he offered.

"Won't work," she said.

"Won't," he said, letting all the Lilliputian protests swarm him frantically, tire themselves into exhausted surrender.

They swapped sets of keys and he put his computer to sleep.

"*I*—could go," he said, but it came out as a question: *should I go?*

"No," she said. "If he sees you he'll just lose it immediately and there'll be no chance. No offense. It's not you it's… him."

So they said I love you at the same time and he left. She looked out from the enormous altitudes, like a climber who has summited but only then sees that this is the wrong mountain, and she recalls all the years she spent trying to ascend the cathedral of limestone, whose steeple, rusted with a faded mint, could not compete with the supreme peak of the AIPOT building. How she had tried to not just believe in but obey the God who hung there, the steeple cross empty but ready, as if awaiting someone else. And she had. She had even opened their home to a prayer meeting, not merely enduring but granting serious thought to the theories of Carla, who filled half the meetings with certainties that eleven years after September eleventh the End would come, eleven being (temporarily) the number of disciples after Judas betrayed—one digit short of completion. Carla's nasal tone, combined with the flagrant way she flared her nostrils as she searched for gestures to match her words, had won over everyone, to the point that even when she missed a meeting no one masked gossip in prayer, suggesting for instance that "we'd really better pray for her, cause we all know she *needs it.*" (Translation: Unlike the rest of us, or at least to a degree that makes our idiosyncrasies borderline virtues, Carla is a crooked line, a troubled lady, a source of anxiety, as how could such a sincere and kind and friendly person, God-fearing, people-loving with a lavishness that puts us to shame, how could such a person be so off kilter of mind?)

And an End *had* come, in two thousand and twelve, as that was the year her now absent eldest came home from having served as acolyte and emptied the snot of his nose on her neck, cleaving and clinging, ringing out his hands with snorts of air, caught air coughed out into her face as he told her what the priest did to the little server boy.

His mother felt the dried snot scattered around her son's

nose, some of it almost bloody from so much crying and the general dry spell that had descended upon the city, her fingers repeatedly running the same patterns on his face, feeling the hardened snot prick like barbs. She pressed her fingers over his ears and said unintelligible things, things indistinct to maybe all but God, who had grown illegible to her in a matter of minutes.

High up here, she remembered what her mother said when she had complained of having too many of the household tasks and chores, the lame and hard ones no one else would do, dished out to her without consent. "Has to be a low for there to be a high." The advice hadn't helped, although she could find no fault with the logic at work in it. But the therapy of perspective was inefficacious, here. Seventeen stories above the crumbs of cars, and the crumbs of the crumbs of walkers, she could not feast on the futility of their comings and goings, the relative equality of those making haste and those moving at a lazy pace. She was at once high and low, already in the basement of the building down the block, the stomach dropped feeling starting already, although she was still, her nose against the glass, if for no other reason than to avoid her reflection's relentless efforts to win her attention, to contain in a mute face all the things she did not need to see, all the things she did not need to know now.

The olive green raincoat she snatched from the lost and found looked ridiculous on her, and it reeked of damp neglect. But it would gain her the several minutes' anonymity, the exact participation in facelessness that she needed to make her way to the front of the crowd, who already moshed gently, as the lowered waters do before the rising tide magnetizes them into an uproar. In this precious gentleness she set to work, pushing others aside, parting them with a breast stroke motion, chin down as she passed the amalgam of angst and strange fear that her aged presence pulled from their pallid faces, letting them know the things she did not need to know now, she could not fully know now, but which they needed to, all of them, every last one, simultaneously pushing them out of the way and leaving them with a touch on the shoulders, as if to say *you're one of mine* to each. Her son's slim magenta pants hardly fit. Watching him squat over the amplifiers, hearing his perfunctory screams, her ears perked. Though on the edges he seemed to emit mere noise, the lower frequencies carried a melody.

Other teenagers took to the stage, two affecting the postureless slunk of the unfazed, one wincing out through the lights and blowing a kiss into the crowd. And as the overture of dissonance resolved itself into a shape she recognized, Keith twisted, with a finesse and a grace not dissimilar to a ballerina's, revealing the university T-shirt he had doctored, so that instead of HARVARD the chest read HATRED.

Without weighing the matter she removed her beret, her red hair spilling out into the yellow light, golden there, impossible to ignore in a sea of heads mostly shaved or died black, except for her son's, whose hair was a clownish puff of orange interrupted by a black line running right down the center, splitting his head in two, trying to celebrate or radiate what, what Keith, what, schizophrenia?, but with the line's precision, the proportionate sides, he could not help but be a cry for what, Keith, come on, son, what? The infinity symbol tattooed around his eyes hypnotized, cut as though by a scissors where the two sides ought to intersect, creating two separate eternities.

Heaven and hell. Her thoughts straddled the extremes as he sang words that did not go with the song the band worked out: "Please allow me to introduce myself, I'm a man of wealth and taste…" Yes, he saw her now. Yes he had to have, how else explain the way his voice descended a key and floundered, feeling for the rungs of the clef but catching on unseen holes that held him down. She retrieved the look she had given him when, three-years old, he would taunt her, begging her to chase him, saying "Me! Catch me!" as she jutted out her jaw and sent him scattering with no more than the suggestion of motion, although she would eventually chase and tackle him, for the ritual that started in ferocity had to have its finale in tickling hilarity.

But this time he did not run. Instead he came closer, flirting with the stage edge and then retracting until he regained balance. His look did not beg. No dog hanging his head after he has trespassed the neighbor's yard again. What gave him that power to deny recognition? What stain, what exhibit of what mother's errors could keep his face so plain, as if his sockets held eyes as unreal as those that ogled out from the eyeless oval atop the evolving, ever-straightening back in *Seven Steps to a Straight Back*?

As the song ended her son ran his hands through the black borderline that cut his head in half, then flared out his green army jacket to reveal three mint-colored orbs hidden on the inside, fastened to his body like sick pustules.

"Tonight you're in for a treat!" he yelled, no longer relying on the microphone to fill the room with his voice. "Let's set the whole city on fire."

The lights had been so low since her entrance that she could not gauge how large the space was, but the number of sheer bodies swelled the room, though each kept barely ascertainable columns of solitude, separated from one another by a kind of metaphysical cellophane.

"We're going to play a little game. A little…" and here he plucked the orbs from his vest the way his dad plucked dead lights from the Christmas tree, when they still had a Christmas tree, "We're going to play a little *roulette*. And while we're having fun we'll do this city a little service. If we win. Blow this place down... Down with all they put up. All the norms they need to keep themselves at the top! Self-serving conventions, am I right?"

A rattle snaked through the room, swelled into a cheer.

"In this game we don't discriminate. Everybody goes with everybody else into... *out of...*" Here he extended his legs a little and began juggling the grenades, which had green dollar faces of dead presidents painted upon them. "One of these three is not like the other. One of 'em 'll blow this fucking building down, damn it into *nothing*. Two'll just fill it with smoke, gag every one out of the place. Shut this city down! And I, your unworthy master of ceremonies—, ladies and gentlemen, I have no idea which is which," he said, still juggling, delighting in his own steadiness. "I... unlike the... I play fair. Chance is the only real way to fairness." With his words he separated the crowd, sending a good two thirds toward the door like atoms smashing, eyes popping and neck veins bulging as some tried to scream but vomited only silence. Others shrilled the building. But a good third remained.

She tried to thumb his number. He would be tucking Zoe into bed. Her fingers numbed against the keys. She tried to count the crowd and got to thirty three before she flung her whole body toward him, her arms and legs extended into an X that tried to both cancel and embrace. Oh God Oh my God please don't let it be the one, she said, ten of the thirty feet that originally divided them still bragging between them as she flung herself into an X again God you are my God don't let it be the one I won't say I'm sorry for leaving you you don't need me isn't the point I'm not an excuse I don't have anything to say except yes I was wrong but so was the one who stole my son was too who thieved literally the whole account of his little soul, who literally left him bankrupt and did so so quickly that the boy didn't even know how to say so, didn't know who could if it was him or you who was bankrupt or both and now God and now God I no God. If I say yes to you will you say no?

Her first leap onto the stage failed, managing only her arm, but the drummer, not knowing who this lady was, dragged her up, taking the microphone and saying, "See, there is no discrimination. Young and old know it's all a big nothing!"

One final time she formed the X and let it fall upon her son.

"It's all a joke. Say it's all a joke," he said, having pulled the plug from one orb, which, aimed at the doorway, enclosed those who remained in a cumulonimbus ominousness, even as it ascended and disseminated throughout the AIPOT building, whispering HSHSHHHHH as it rose.

Then she spit into his mouth, holding down his hands as she did so, muscles made strong from scouring the gunge and filth for hours beyond account, circling the base of the toilet, the borders of sinks, the lips of a refrigerator that coughed as she did now, scanning peripherally for glimpses of bodies, catching one going slack in the arms of an upright one, spitting again and again, startling him with stings until she could dredge only spittle, until his nonchalance, which he had maintained for so long, gave way to a cringe, and then a quick flinch of his fist.

"I'll speak a little," she said, willing her voice into a kind of croon, watching the twitches around his eyes disappear, the fear there that wrinkled under the rage. "You're not this," she said, as other members of the band felt for the remaining orbs like stubborn insects bent on the bait even as the poison consumes them. "This is not you."

"I am," he said, "It is. That's the whole point. Can't pick and choose. I am what you don't want to see. *This* is me."

"You don't *lose* if you give up," she said.

"This whole thing's... no one wins no matter what," he flung at her, her spit still gargling in his throat. "How'd you—

why come here? What'd you show up?" His voice sunk into a low, hollow calm as the last stage lights flickered out.

"Did I? It wasn't me, really. Was it?"

"Aw, not this again, Mom. Shit on this stop it stop it—*no!*" he spat. "Doesn't show up millions of other times. Don't pull out that old card anymore. Old Father, artificer, hold him close to your chest. Keep him to yourself, now," and, his hands hastening to cover ears torn by the dead guitar's ricocheted dissonance and reverb, he said, "Really, real sorry for what I'm about to do. Better one die than many... but the whole point was bring down the city. The whole building or something." And, shoving her back, he pulled out the pustule and nabbed the pin out casually, slowly, the way his dad yanked toothpicks out of a tin.

And as the microphone breathed in their words and shot them voluminous, past the wall of glittering, obsidian smoke, louder than the HSHSHHHHHHH and the fire alarm, out into the unseen, she shoved him down, and he clung to her like a ship-wrecked passenger to a shard of wood, floating there in the dark, on the deep, chafed by what he held onto but lifted up by it just the same. And other words breathed there, in the air, between the joints and the marrow lifted, between soul and spirit spiraling out, words severing the two like a surgeon's steady orders, and one went down and down and down again while the other slipped up and was swallowed by the grave and graying smoke. And the whetted words returned to the wounded surgeon's mouth, escaping by some other exit.

Pawned

AFTER THE CHILDREN MOVED OUT he developed this new way of it. Always as though playing a timed game of chess, but instead of trying to capture his opponent's rook or checkmate his opponent, somehow it was as if he was using his queen to gather every pawn on the board, regardless of side, and present them all before a king that was clearly not *his*.

But when I lived with him and loved him in the coffee house hours of youth, Christmas lights on the walls and twenty-five intensive conversations caffeinated into assents and eventual declines around us, he would change the rules, collapsing the conventions of the game in hair-pulling fits, his brow furrowed there, underneath the lamp that always dangled above us but whose light could not illuminate his sallow, shadowed face. Sometimes, if his loss seemed sure, he would overturn the chess-board with one cool sweep; his hand struck down each player with absolute detachment. And then he would look you straight in the eye, all cool while he set out the pieces again, and as you took it all in you saw that he was one move away from cornering your king. Other times he would make obvious mistakes that you couldn't believe he had committed without other, hidden strategies—malevolent or benign. The way a father lets his child win in order to pique a young one's dedication to the game. Or was it something else entirely? Sacrifice the queen to preserve a pawn. Redeem a pawn for another pawn. Things which led, indirectly, to so many losses, but which never seemed to trouble him.

And I? I can't help but ask, lame platitude it may be: what was I in his game? Is it even right of me to call the game *his*? Was it *ours*? After all, didn't I play? If you knew him you'd know that my claiming I was a pawn in his hand isn't saying much at all, may even mean he loved me above all the rest. If he did, I never knew it. Or—did I? What I did know was this: even when he won he sensed, always, that on some other plane he was the perpetual loser and so never—not once in all our countless rounds— did he give way to hands-held-high, histrionic celebration. At any given time there were two games going on at once, see. *See*, you see, you see me now?

Yes, yes he defeated me countless times. But—you don't know this the way that *I* do and no one, outside of him, ever will: in another way he was beaten badly, badly, too many times and too long for any man, and never lost that admirable muscle of his mind.

So here I am. And he is gone. And I'll stay here till he returns, though somehow I find myself moving towards the door, heading towards the pawn shop, to buy that old chessboard back, the one I pawned yesterday for a crinkled green rectangle, solemn Abe Lincoln looking up at me pleadingly. Last night was a bad one. Woke up seven times. At dawn I dealt a deck of cards across our king-sized bed, laid out the start of a solitaire game in the spot where he used to sleep. Found it's a game I could never get used to. I will pay them the ten dollars the tag asks. I will look them in the face with a loser's bleary eyes. I've done a lot of low things in life, but I never bought cheap only to sell dear. Still, for the one I love, for the lost one, I will play their game.

Their Fire is Not Quenched

The only hope, or else despair
Lies in the choice of pyre or pyre—
To be redeemed from fire by fire.
—T. S. Eliot, *Four Quartets*

REST ASSURED, Allan always had the last word. Moving the overstimulated houseplant out of the way, his left hand did not know what his right hand—which gesticulated like a fanatical football devotee—was doing. He had fertilized the jonquils to offset dirtied snow, give the gloom some shoots of life, but the leaves had grown with reckless ambition. Their gold-tipped green blocked his view of the blue screen. Like a middle-aged child to an elderly parent, the TV talked at a very high volume. And Allan talked back.

Winter had lasted too long. At the base of the bay window, orbs of blue frost still mingled with smudges—fingerprint evidence that he had been a child once. He felt bad for the plant, sure that it would wilt so close to the cold. But he had to *see* the commentators, had to thrill with the news found only in their faces.

Plant aside, Allan gave rapt attention to the small screen television, a geriatric model that sat across from him at the small table. He gestured as though what he watched could watch back. Whenever the experts explained what was wrong with the world,

Allan listened just long enough to find grounds for a groan. And then he talked over them, testing their twenty minute newscast with his filibuster temperament. One day he would tell the heads what to talk about. As the show reached denouement, a hysterical syncretism of international voices chanted "Our Global Village," accompanied by a synthesizer's sanguine flute.

Allan clicked off the TV. Every time he did it sounded like a fuse burnout—*ffclatk!* He surveyed the silent room, flattening bubbles in the red-checkered table cloth. Old breadcrumbs continued to harden, waiting for birds to peck them away. Dad liked his toast black, lathered with more butter than bread. He spooned butter into his coffee, too, as it kept him from hunger until dinnertime. When Allan wiped the tabletop, which he hadn't done in living memory, a greasy substance coated his hand. Margarine! Mom must have made the swap at some point, trying to get Dad to eat the replica. He now found that most of it had ended up on the table. Dad's antennae had detected it.

The whole kitchen cried out for a good cleaning. His right hand had tipped the clay orange pot. The plant reasserted its ambition even as its soil trailed across the table, leaving its roots exposed. People live in worse conditions. Visions of the global village. High rise tenements like metal honeycombs. Lean huts in the third world. But this only bought him ten seconds of content. Feeling the tremens, he cursed the dirt and changed the channel. His lips twitched when the screen blazed with News You Can Use.

Allan lived alone. He had assumed his childhood home when his mother "fell asleep" in her easy chair. Mom had died just days after Dad. She hadn't seemed sick, but was always a follower. Strange how commonplace it seemed, her passing where she collapsed at day's end for decades, raising their "gang of nine." That was what the neighbors called them. His mother Rita possessed a fidgety confidence. When anyone commented on her ample brood she would clutch her purse tightly and then unclasp it, digging inside for a few pennies and pressing them in their hands. Or, if their fingers resisted, she would simply let the coins clang like cymbals, spinning in unruly circles at their feet. *A penny for your funnies,* she would say.

His mother had meant to live as far away from the pollutions of the city as she could, but as her husband had been unable to finish college before their third child emptied the savings, she endured the little bungalow on the bus line. At least then she could keep the car, flit out to the country like a fresh-air addict. She did this until they had eight (Allan, Anna, Becca, Joseph, Leah, Stephen, Tobit, Zechariah), straining the law, squeezing two to a seatbelt. When they reached a bluff at the end of a field she would release them and watch them go wild. Allan remembered her laugh, which followed him into the Switchgrass.

For fifty years her husband Cody took the 30 Z to J. F.'s Padlocks, watching boards replace windows as he went down the line. He took Allan with him sometimes, when school was out and Mom was done in. Dad would peer over his shoulder when the bus let them off at the once-wooden gates. Early on, Padlocks was bought out by a bigger vendor. Barbed wire and steel replaced flutes and grooves. The place assumed a new name, Hobbes' Security Specialists, but everyone called it "Padlocks." It had been so for a hundred years. Each day Dad vanished behind this fortress into the factory, his friendly eyes decoys for the dour visions that danced through his head.

Once, when Rita returned from a jut to a family farm, the trunk full of beef chunks wrapped in newspaper, she pattered around the kitchen like a strutting hen. No more, she told Cody. No more would she live with her children like chickens, cramped in this pen of a godforsaken city. She handed him a cabbage bigger than his head.

"Many people in this world live on a lot less, in rooms far smaller, with leakier roofs," he said. But before he went to bed he dug out the ad for correspondence classes. The paper, now a bookmark in his Bible, still smelled of the rum he had spilled on it a year before. Cody squeezed his eyes to read the details. COLLEGE MADE CONVENIENT! LEARN FROM THE PRIVACY OF YOUR HOME AT YOUR OWN PACE! He could not—temples throbbing his eyes shut—read the rest. Besides, the font size rivaled the footnotes that explained the Scriptures to him. Impossible to squint sense from.

Next morning he went into work early and wandered around the walkway of the main plant's perimeter, a warden overseeing an empty prison. He paced not a little that day. As though reading the sweat that filled the lines of his palms, two days later his boss's boss, Gary Husk, called him in. "You need a bigger pond," he said, and promoted Cody to supervisor of supervisors. "Watchman of the watchmen," he used to joke. The work left him famished for tangible things, but he stayed on until retirement, growing more otherworldly with each passing election year.

Allan checked the mail, though he knew it wasn't due for a few hours. Finding none, he retreated into the kitchen. He sopped up the golden ooze of his over-easy eggs, a task that took twice as long because the moody toaster had hardened the bread. Worse than Dad's. It came out less like a sponge and more like a bad mop—the kind that reroutes stains but does not remove them. Plate lined with refuse, Allan's stomach gurgled. More. He turned on the TV again. *Ffclatk!*

Over the sudden agitation he heard the heat ducts' raspy exhale—rattling, yet reliable. During News You Can Use with Jack Atlantis he felt a rash of hot flush through his body. Caught in a back-and-forth with Atlantis over whether the U.S. should arm the rebels, bomb the chemical plants, or retreat from the Middle East, Allan had thought this hot flash the familiar derivative of a lively debate—*Bush or Carter doctrine?* was the quandary's clear subtext, the question too expert for the dumbed-down populace. Allan rifled through the junk drawer, found the penlight his bank AIPOT had sent him. *Your business is ours.* The slogan unsettled him, but the bulb was bright. Descending the steep and narrow stairs that led to the basement, he remembered the tussle in Dad's last days, when the old man had declined to fix the furnace.

Ω

"The thing's older than me," he had said. "Let it die in peace." As if you could live without heat in Milwaukee. Dad turned over in the bed, buried under four blankets. He did not have the monies and he did not have the know-how, he said into the mattress.

"Plenty of people in this world live without enough heat," Dad had said in the morning, exiting the room and returning with a second flannel, a washed out purple one that mismatched the blue and brown one underneath. Then he shoved his hands deep into his pockets and looked between two wall-hung frames—President Reagan and Saint Rita. He left, and a door slam from the bowels of the house shook its frame. Dad came in stooped under two blankets, balanced them like woodpiles on his back. He set the downy covers at the feet of his wife, who passed the thicker one to her son. Dad folded his hands and went away.

That night Dad had spat hard while brushing his teeth and he fell into a coughing spell that lasted fifteen minutes. Allan, the only one of the nine who had moved back home, had muted the TV, resenting Anna and Becca, Joseph and Leah, Stephen and Tobit and especially Zechariah. Even the untalented ones had made names for themselves, displaced across the States. No one close enough to help him care. No one failure enough to be stuck at home, living with the dying. As Dad hacked on, he turned off Foreign Affairs: *Realpolitik* Uncensored. Knocking on the bowed bathroom door without waiting for an answer, he pushed in. Dad lacked the gravity conferred by his black framed glasses. They had fallen with his toothbrush, settling in contortion at the base of the sink. Scum-covered. His father's liver-yellow eyes looked like the bottom-dwelling catfish in the family aquarium. Swiveling slowly below the lime green light that lit the tank's upper half, that fish always clung to the mildewed floor. At feedings, the rest vacuumed up the food, left him only those flakes they didn't notice. If you stood there watching while all of this occurred he would ogle you, cusses buried behind his eyes, blaming you and the universe for the others' successes.

Dad pushed him out of the bathroom. "I can take care of myself," he said, nasally.

He was the same, the same Dad who had enrolled his sons in a survival youth camp. SMALL-"a"-APOCALYPSE. Dad dropped them in a circle of dust at an unmapped field edge, the car rolling slowly as he shouted curt sendoffs. Then he threw the car in reverse and shoved three army surplus sleeping bags—"We don't have the money for another. And besides, in times of survival you won't have all that you wished you did, but you learn to make due"—through the half-cracked window. "Remember," he yelled, "there's no need to be troubled about The End... We just have to be realistic about the end of the world as it is," revving the wide brown station wagon and imparting sad rearview eyes that disclosed something coded. Allan felt for his canteen when his swallow closed on a dry throat, but he resisted, unsure whether the water would last the weekend.

When Allan left for college at seventeen—"Our brood's smart-pants," Mom would say—he stayed away until he finished his doctorate in political science. He dissertated on exoteric rhetoric. The policies of State must stay quiet. They can stay the same across generation, but administrations must read the signs of the times, altering their explanations accordingly. While it had worked for a while to say that our Middle East presence was mandated by *raison d'état*, the "mere security" would not work on tomorrow's voters, moralizers who would need to be told grander things. We're arming freedom fighters, imparting democracy to a backward, brutal people. Tinkering through policies and timetables and talking points—all of this titillated Allan like nothing else. He fell asleep seeing himself seated at the head of an ovular table, turning manipulations of data into dreams of a new world order. His father's nuclear nightmares would rest in peace, as dead as the trajectories of history they fed on.

And now here he was, a tenant with his parents at thirty, waiting for East Coast Think Tanks to read his resume and recognize him. NOS (Novus Ordo Speculations) was an especially likely hire. He had spent a summer in New York, interning under George Friedens, NOR's Director. Friedens was brilliant but his political shtick was passé—a Henry Kissinger kind of naked inhumanity, a total disregard for naysayers, all of this combined with an unseemly informality among insiders: pen biting and absent-minded marks on the white board, marks of a skeletal nervousness, weird fears at his marrow. Still, the bones stood more sturdily than most of the other tanks, teetering things. "Tin tankards," Friedens called them, and he hawed a high-octave laugh.

When Dad finally came out of the bathroom, he nodded and grinned as though nothing had happened. His dad's eyes, dilated wide, disagreed with his diminished body, which seemed smaller in the hallway mirror. Seeing himself small beside his son, Cody committed a barely discernible cringe. Allan's poor posture had produced scalene shoulders, but his husky frame still filled the mirror. Dad turned back into the bathroom and filled the sink with more phlegm, and Allan followed him in. He kept his left hand on the sink edge to angle his father up, his right reaching for the dropped glasses before it shot back and caught his dad by the collar, muscling his seat atop the unused walker, unemployed in the bathroom, looking like a discarded high chair. Cody, coughing both by necessity and to give the tears in his eyes another cause, felt for his son, fingers splayed in terror. Finally, Allan fumbled his fingers through the old man's, hoisting him upright. Dad's head smelled faintly of shoe polish. Peppered by the bathroom light's on-and-off flicker, the liver spots that blotched his father's forehead formed a mosaic lock. Unable to speak, Dad summoned all his strength to point at the glasses, which his son dragged out of the scum, rinsed, and rested on his nose. Allan looked into the toilet for a long time. Flicking his fingers like a mute infant, his father indicated a black comb. He ran it through the old man's seven remaining strands of hair. Try as he might, he couldn't straighten the curls of barbed wire that clung to the old man's skull.

When they emerged, one dragging and the other shuffling, through the warped frame of the bathroom door, Allan searched his mother's eyes, hankering for reflections of the TV blue. He found them closed, caught a small stream of drool at the edge of her mouth, saw her hearing aids switched off and scattered on the oblong coffee table propped up with grayed hay and tall grass—the spoils of a visit to the country. He knew what he had to do.

Inching Dad along with angled exertions of his hip, Allan brought him into his parent's room. Hoisting his dad's dangling body, he yanked the Murphy wallbed down. Allan lowered the lanky torso and then lifted up the limbs. Dad's whole body was limp, corpselike. The full moon illuminated the old red phone, showed its frayed but still firing wires.

"Do you want me to call for a doctor, Dad?" he asked.

"Don't you dare let me die like a—dog under a microscope," his father shot back. "I'm not a specimen—I'm a child of God."

Allan waited until the breaths, though shallow, had the same number of seconds between them. Only once, when he counted to ten waiting for the wearied chest to rise once more, did he reach for the red phone. A startled suck through heavy phlegm. A squirm of consciousness scanned the room from slitted eyes, but gravity pressed harder than usual on his warped frame. Allan slipped his pointer through the flannel seam, felt the beating jugular. Lost to sleep, his dad swatted it as Allan had those massive mosquitoes that seemed to bite through the bug net at SMALL "a" APOCALYPSE. But then, with panicked reaches, Dad beckoned the hand back. His son, who waved away all of the sentimental aureoles that tried to toss themselves around the moment, surrendered to the internment. At last, just after he had acclimated to his imprisonment, his father raised his head and said, "The market's been hard on this house. Hit us hard. Why I gave up. Wonder who'll run the real estate where I'm going. Two possibilities. The greatest slum lord in the whole of the world. Or to dwell with the one who had no place to rest when he was here." And then he rallied and left the room, his smooth steps all calm.

Allan eyed the steel sign that crowned the old wooden crucifix. *INRI.* It read like a think tank acronym. Their parish had tossed it in the trash, and Tobit had discovered it after Mass. The lean Jesus had a thirsty look. *It must have been like that.* Allan thought of the Baghdad prison where a Sergeant and his soldiers had crucified an Iraqi criminal. *Politics ruined by rhetoric. S.O.B. leakers and lousy state rhetoric.*

Dad returned with another flannel. That winter lasted forever. Allan did not pound on his father's chest. He did not fall into Dad's arms, dizzied by a reel of black and white memories. No. He picked up the red phone. Speaking with the dispatcher, he appreciated her clinical tone. That sound was what he strove for. It was the sound of those who saw things as they are.

Or—and the thought swooped down and pecked at his mind's eye, quick like a killer hawk—was it that he could not surpass the chill? If you spent years pouring over politics you had to make yourself hard. He ricocheted the puck of remorse across the frozen floor.

Allan had tried to accept his father's piety—a quiet kind that rarely reared its unreason—the way he had his youngest sister's fantasy football league. Good humor could go a long way. Everyone was given to imaginings. True, the God his dad inherited— and tweaked liberally to meet his own needs—led the man to waste many hours that could have been better spent, but as long as he gave most of his being to pragmatic decisions that did not shirk the harshness and contingencies of reality, these little otherworldly sprees were relatively harmless, and maybe even useful, if they kept him freed from other pursuits that could compromise the interests of state. Besides, even the honest mind could not ceaselessly face the unforgiving facts, facts whose full complexity most of us never even see, given the newsman's need—a yield of his own realism—to break the yolks and fry them over nice and easy instead of serving them up raw, shells and all, saying, stiffly, "Swallow." The brutal truth demanded that he declare his father a follower, and one had to deal with followers and rulers according to discordant codes. Every great ruler needed to ensure that nothing escaped his lips that would dispose one to think him impious. No. Even Allan folded his hands at dinner, nodding his head on holidays, the embodiment of mercy, good faith. The appearance of religion covered a multitude of sins for the princes of this world. Failure to achieve it placed one's power in peril.

As he smoothed his father's still-warm lids until they blanketed his pupils, Allan saw how poorly he had practiced this maxim. He knew—a ruthless knowing enlarged each time his father looked at him, still more ruthless in that his father never said these things outright—that he embodied none of these things. He did not call Father Powers, whose black bag and candles would only upset the quietude. Walking to the dresser, he stood there for a long time, watching the Christ in the mirror. Vinegar. He could do better. He found the bottle of codeine, buried under self-help pamphlets, pension payments, and a Novena for Hopeless Cases. Seeing it, he knew his mother had prayed it for him. Allan shook his head like a man who, selling meat at market, refuses the offered price. His father's cough killed his nerves—crackling with ache, wracked with death. Standing over Dad he split the pill and, when the coughing fit finished, poured the powder on his tongue. He would wait until morning to tell his mother. Let her rest in peace one last night, clonked out in her easy chair beside the big window.

Earlier that day his mother made much ado over a rare dinner. The parish priest, Father Powers, was paying them a visit. Although she had not done so for several years, that morning his mother had haunted one of her old farms. She did it, she said, "to test God, to see if he's really punishing me like this." Her license had been revoked for regularly running stop lights— "You're a danger to yourself and others, ma'am." When she had thawed the half-frozen shank of beef even her taxed eyes could see that the white lines of suet were fatter than they had been. When she made her signature roast all those years ago, she had to add only a small army of potatoes as padding. The shanks stretched well, always feeding eleven bellies, and oftener a neighbor or two, too—a floppy kid found propped on some ramshackle chair, mouth full of peas.

As she peeled the far smaller pile of russets she found them pimpled with more black spots than before. This would not be a bother but for the priest's visit. She had invited him, Allan knew, as a kind of payment—to offset her account with "the Lord." Mom said that visiting the farm felt more like an act of charity this time, as though in going she was dropping off a few nails to help prop up a declining house. "Like the Yourricks. You remember the Yourricks? Your dad donated all their locks. We paid for half the lumber. It would have been too hard to watch that family fall." Allan, not immune to his Mom's proclivity toward penance, had accompanied her "in case a cop comes, we can switch seats real quick." "Why don't I just drive, Mom?" "If I let you take over these things, in a week I'll be bedbound. Have ta keep purpose, Al."

She left with a rush of fine feeling that led to her foot feeding the gas and skinning the side of a trailer chockfull of cows, their eyes as black as potato pimples. *Guardian angel saved me maybe on account of my doing all this for the priest who was coming to dinner.* Allan the clairvoyant could read her little mind.

"Like people," Allan heard her say over the peeler's persistent snips. "Potatoes. Bruise them and they grow thicker skin to protect themselves."

For the most part, Father Powers had decent vision. As he was their priest, his parents had invited Powers over once before, when he assumed St. Tertullian's a decade ago. Stretched across two other parishes—"dying gems in the city's gut"—the priest had the lean, thirsty look of the Christ who hung permanently in his parent's room.

Father Powers seemed to nod. That is, as Allan exhibited expertise on policy, the priest appeared to approve of his answers to China and Israel, Immigration and Denuclearization—the necessary evil of the Middle East.

"Don't our own theologians have something to say about that, Father?"

"What's that?"

"Necessary evils," Allan said.

The man was badly in need of sleep. Nearly yawning, he downed the boxed merlot. His mother had really outdone herself. God. Allan felt bad for the priest. Clearly committed to the people, he could have been a community organizer. Unlike too many politicos, Allan knew the necessity of grassroots. So long as America had a whimper of democracy remaining, these bottom-up riots would rise from the bottom feeders. It was a matter of how to channel their resentment. They just needed to be tended better, very well-watered and then, when elections came, burned. He almost broached the subject with the priest, but he knew the bleeding heart would attack when he told him what "burned" meant.

The only territories in which Father's theories turned naïve were Heaven and Hell. When he spoke of them, his fork suspended with four stabbed peas, three of which slid down to the plate by the time he finished, he stared straight ahead as though his rheumy eyes saw the Infernal Fires and Empyrean Spheres at once. Allan tried to reroute the conversation's backwards caravan by bringing up the border wall, but Father Powers, looking directly at him to let him know he had heard him, turned to Rita and asked.

"And how is your bodily health?"

"We're looking for someone to cut the lawn, Father. We had a man—highly recommended by the Benzes, you know the Benzes, from the parish?—come by last month and when he was done he handed us a bill for fifty dollars. If that doesn't cry out to heaven for vengeance! Cody was always the one to take care of it. At least since the last of our little ones skipped the state. Not that I blame them. No jobs. What life could they live here? It's not a large yard. Trust me. When all nine were here they couldn't be out there at once without a fight coming five minutes later. Not enough space." When, instead of answering, Father chewed the fat inside his cheek and, turning to Allan, made the gesture in the painting at the back of the parish. Pilate's hand extended in an exorbitant *Ecce Homo*.

"Not that I'm complaining, Father," his mother added when Allan gripped his butter knife.

For five decades Mom had fought every itch to carp. After about twenty years of slipping, typically through contained but violent venting in the presence of the whole family, at the end of dinner, she had come up with a mechanism of compromise that allowed her to siphon all discontent into one location. Bleeding agreeableness in the face of adversities large and small during thirteen of the fourteen waking hours of her day, she kept a private devotion—a mere sixty minutes—withdrawing into the closet in her bedroom. Phone cord stretched taut, audible to no one, letting her voice cook and crescendo, she called her friend Carol and together they commiserated and competed, comparing their respective records of the day's absurdities, each assuring the other that life ought to be how she said, that what she said was true—that too many mishandled the talents that God had ungrudgingly given them. She emerged from the closet, beaming, descending from the mountain to sweep and vacuum with élan.

Allan knew, at night sometimes, that he took his mother for granted, but he knew, too, that she could do better. Too much wasted on blind alleys, peccadilloes. Obsessions obese with small-mindedness.

"For the love of God, can you go down and throw some more pellets in the stove, Allan?" Dad said, knife rattling repeatedly against the plate until he managed to puncture a burnt chunk of potato with the blade. Allan knew the cantankerous hue of the words came from the difficulty the old man had with breathing. But did the priest? Allan searched the visitor's face, found traces of pity everywhere. Elevated eyebrows and lowered chin.

An infection had led to twenty percent of Cody's lungs being removed, not to mention the rheumatism that, ever present, vacillated between mildly irritating and riotous. The bills to treat these illnesses were what kept them drinking boxed wine.

"Just a second, Dad," he said. Allan sliced a grape into three and chewed each piece with patience. Rising, he studied the wallpaper cows, blue and smiling and chewing contentedly, stuck there with the cross's same permanence. They mocked him with their mirth. He held his side. Allan took offense at his Dad's sharp tone. The priest's presence meant that this familiar sin, "venial" enough in private, was more than mere personal offense. Public humiliation.

Too embarrassed to say "I'm not a child to be ordered around," he lifted a dense black suitcoat from the back of his chair and assumed it like a mantle, priestly in the sacrificial character of his stride. Out of their sight, he heard his mother say, "He tried to cut the grass three times since he's been home. Every time he ends up in bed for half a day afterward. Awful allergies."

"Better that than it being a problem of the will," the priest said, delicately interrupting her sympathetic sigh. "Many, many cases of children—children! What am I saying? These kids are in their twenties and thirties!—returning home and treating their parents like butlers and maids. I hear of these things with increasing frequency."

Halted in the stuffy hallway, a middle finger of angst scratched its nail into Allan's spine, and on the way downstairs he halted before the cove—previously home to the family telephone—where his father kept opened the Bible. The thin pages wouldn't burn for long, but they would catch more quickly than the cereal boxes his father set aside for kindling. Spreading his fingers out and letting them drag down the grooves of the wainscoting, he moved on.

By the time Allan returned, Father Powers was sustaining a lean that seemed to require the strictest obedience of his every muscle and nerve. Suspended there across the table, his ear was a mere foot from Cody's mouth. Cody, who even at full volume was almost indistinguishable from a mime, cut short his confidences when Allan again appeared at the table. He gave his son a smile that seemed mischievous, cleared his throat and gasped out, "Allan's going to be ordering the known world someday, Father, so you'd better make sure you get on his good side if the Church expects to keep receiving those clauses on religious liberty."

The priest, seeing the funny bone at the base of Cody's muscled facetiousness, let out a polite laugh that he seemed to regret, seemed to want back, to spend on a better occasion. "Yes, Cody, but you know my major concern is a variant of yours: that the folks they have supervising the torments of hell are more ruthless and let loose than Abu Ghraib or Guantanamo in its 'glory days.' I hear the devilish overseers of the demonic minions rally their troops by blowing trumpets out of their asses!"

Allan covered his mouth with two fingers. Father Powers answered the father's interrupted confidences, but eyed the son: "It seems that what troubles you most is the question of the eternal fires. Whether fires, which can—obviously—burn the flesh, can—not so obviously—scald the soul. The permanence of such a state is also a classic tripping wire, a common mine on the field of metaphysical questions. St. Augie has reams to say on the problem, but maybe the heart of the matter is this" (and here he reached into the black bag from which two pale candles peeked, and, pretending to fall under the weight of the book his fingers flipped through, he read): "The soul, then, is pained with the body in that part where something occurs to hurt it; and it is pained alone, though it be in the body, when some invisible cause distresses it, while the body is safe and sound. Even when not associated with the body it is pained; for certainly that rich man was suffering in hell when he cried, 'I am tormented in this flame.' The salamander outlives his exposure to fire…"

The teapot, which had been whistling shyly on the stove-top, shrieked.

"Will you have some Earl Grey, Father?" Rita asked, nodding *yes* on his behalf. "I've got lemons galore!" Lifting a finger as if to plead for a pause in the conversation, she departed and returned with a jar of unlabeled teabags, some of them suspiciously familiar to Allan from twelve years earlier. When his mother reached through the black tea dust that had leaked through the bags, when her claw—had she cut her nails this year?—ascended with an individually-wrapped bag, Allan stopped scratching his ribs.

At the end of the evening, after Father Powers had finished with relish three large cups of tea, he asked if he could see the pellet stove. The rectory furnace was getting old. Did a stove like that make the air drier than a machine that runs on gas? If they did not mind, about how much does one of these cost per month? Besides wood pellets, would he need to regularly purchase anything else? Allan, who had asked to be excused an hour earlier in order to "take care of some things," could not maintain his computer clicks that, like winged feet, carried him out of his parent's flyover home. He pressed his ear to the heat vent, spraining his neck to hear.

They were good people, he insisted, chiding himself for not emerging to help his father to bed. Good people. Whatever that means. And then he heard the priest's garrulous laugh, which was not garrulous but dense with a deep good cheer. Allan chastised himself for blacklisting the priest into a caricature. The Founding Fathers had found it necessary to preserve the idea of hell, too. The threat of eternal perdition exercised a salutary influence on public morals. They come in all kinds. It was just a matter of knowing what was needed to govern each one. Father Powers was making a joke about the parish having plenty of awful hymnals that he would be delighted to gainfully employ as kindling.

Ω

The obnoxious rasp had grown into the swansong of his day's plans. Having descended the stairs, he felt his nose dry immediately. The air was unbearable. A suctioning, agitated hot. He had cut his palm on the corroded padlock that kept the pellet stove closed. But it was open now, and he was craning his head into its hot belly.

It is important to shape circumstances before crises emerge. Allan remembered—and almost recited—that line from the Statement as his nostrils twitched. This close to the stove, he was sure that this decrepit old cauldron had hastened his father's passing. The codeine was just a lubricant, grease to make the passage easier. And then there was the priest's talk of hellfire. That would shorten anyone's lifespan.

The stove coughed. The young man who had done the inspection had said something about all the gunk stuck in the vents, how fast air filters wore out with this kind of "heating device." "I don't mean to make you sick," he had said, "but think of it like this. Stuck in those vents are millions of little flakes of human skin—little cells of flesh just whirling around and around the house. A new heating system would clean them out so you could breathe easy." Like his father, Allan had smelled the salesman swimming in the young man's skin, and it had made his own crawl. But standing here, feeding shredded cereal boxes into the dead ash heap, he could not quash the possibility that the inspector had more than his own interest in mind. Still, for now, he needed to feed this cauldron thing. It seemed to be whining for lack of food. The cereal cardboard was too thick to catch fire. Absent the blue heart that sometimes pulsed at its core, the pellet stove contained a few sand grains of orange. Nothing more. How it was so hot down here he could not figure.

Allan's eyes hunted the plain gray basement for more promising fodder. What fantasies had possessed his mother to make her preserve these shelves of rot? Mop heads donning blackened frills of cloth hung from the ceiling like the hair of her daughters dangling from the backyard monkey bars. A chore chart in the shape of a clock occupied the space once owned by a hideous pastoral thrift store painting his mother had bought for the frame. From sequin pins his mother had forged the letters G-O-D I-S A-L-W-A-Y-S W-A-T-C-H-I-N-G. He ripped off the chart and, feeling its thinness, a flimsy film of hope lifted his spirits. The clock had nine hands, each with a child's name, each pointing to a specific chore. His name aimed at Cleaning Up. After holding the well-preserved chart against the orange grains, then using it as a broom to gather the scattered dots of hot into the center, he gave up, then remembered.

With long lunges—three, four steps at a time—the kind that propelled him when his mother called them for dinner, he ascended the stairs, catching the door handle at the top and so barely finding his balance there. Without looking, he reached around the corner into the cove that used to keep the family telephone. Although reams of paper stood on call in the hallway closet, only the Bible would do.

First—and although he only half confessed this test to himself—he ripped out the dedication page of his father's Bible. He reeled back, blinking. Was the paper immune, preserved, protected? Would God hasten his death? Suddenly, he knew the horror the POWs had felt when those dissident soldiers burned their Qur'an. Needless. Another blemish on the American face. But still he somehow now knew them. His father. The mujahidin. His mother. Father Powers. He would need to reconsider the role of religion in foreign policy. To study all the sacred books. To pass through some sort of test. Burn a copy of Machiavelli, maybe. That would give a taste. And then to be purged of residual superstition—what little remained. His head felt heavy, hollowed out lead filled with water. Afraid.

As soon as these terrors escaped the page lit up, an artery of blue amplifying so fast that, reaching out as though against his will, he nearly burned his hand. And then it collapsed. Unthinkingly, like a master struck by a slave, he hit back. Genesis. Exodus. Page by page he rebuilt the blaze.

The laugh that left Allan's lungs came out garrulous, so different from any noise he had previously produced that he even felt a single coal of fear char the blue beauty that filled the belly of the stove. What? God. Right in front of his face, a pellet sack slumped like a shot soldier. He heaved the pellet on his shoulder and felt his strength suspending its weight. The little pills of wood poured out in a spray, like a cataract of water from a firefighter's hose, and when he was finished the room went cold. After a long moment he touched the stove edges and, finding them mild, stuck his head inside. Hells bells. The words rung in his head. Hell's belly. Hell.

"Ah, hell." The words burned down from his brain to his tongue and then disappeared into time.

Allan lowered a cot from the ceiling, one of his brothers' old beds, and shoved it next to the hottest part of the furnace. Though visited by an uncompromising weariness, he forced himself upstairs. He was emptying the bank to pay for this cell phone, but at least he could catch the news through its cracked, frosted screen. He needed it more in case they called from New York. NOS. He burned to share with someone his insights—the primacy of religion in American foreign policy.

He woke at midday to find the fire not quenched.

Impossible. Irritated, with a tamed but determined gait, he stepped outside. The April air brushed him with faint memories of frost. He pressed his palm hard against the water faucet. With an agitated toddler's grasp, Allan unwound the long green garden hose and forced it into the basement. At the bottom of the stairs he loosened the nozzle and let the water torrent into the stove. Even when the rains he made reached his knees the fire was not quenched. The belly of the stove was at the level of his chest. He could not dial for help. He had soaked the cellphone and all the circuits had snapped. The dispatcher would not believe him. Not to mention the mortification. Allan looked one last time, only to find the explosion of undying sparks still roiling in the pellet stove, ordered into no constellations—armed rebels self-imploding into stars that railed against his comprehension. He closed his eyes but he found them there, too, their light filling the darkened inside of his lids. Their fire was not quenched.

Natural Causes

THE AIPOT (American International Pecuniary Oligarchy of Transactions, formerly Union of Transactions Ordered for the Pecuniary Improvement of America) co-head of the sub-division of Private Investment Services &—but we had better omit his exact Transactional Subspecies in order to avoid becoming an object of litigious indignation—said they had planned to give the young man the position, and even let the camera close in on the letter of offer, which was dated the day of the intern's death.

A thumbprint blur hid the face of the co-head of the sub-division of Private Investment Services &—, his voice doctored by digital magic that bestowed a handsome anonymity: "The fact is, and I'll be candid with you," the co-head said, offering his frankness as if it were frankincense, "this is new territory for us. We're just used to working with ambitious people who have high stamina, and, lacking that, normally nobody makes it even this far in the intern stage. So there's a kind of self-selection *out,* a natural kind of way to cut and keep personnel we can count on. These are people, *we* are people who *want* to over-perform.

"But I can tell you AIPOT's response has been above and beyond. This single incident sparked immediate global review, and through a key card system we're now monitoring how many hours each employee or intern works in a row, to the point that an alarm will go off every time AIPOT's central intelligence recognizes someone's been in office for two twelve hour shifts in under forty-eight hours. Now look, it's not—we can't—the laws of the industry can't just *change*"—here he snapped his fingers and turned to stare out the high-rise window, eyes lidded with an odd fusion of anxiety and confidence that leaked through even the ovular blur obscuring his face—"it's not as though we can force people, in an authoritative manner, to stop working. Which goes back to my initial point. Believe me, we feel bad for the kid, very badly, actually, and his family, too. We do. And we're doing a global review—the whole world, literally everywhere we have a bank, all in response to this single kid. So it's serious. But we can't—quite frankly the banking industry'd collapse if we blanket-capped cumulative hours."

A drove of journalists peppered the man with competing questions which congealed into a horrible noise, like the laugh of a robotic hyena.

"So sorry—have to go. Last thing I wanted to mention, though, is that the kid died of natural causes. I mean to say I know his decision—and remember, even though I understand that he felt pressured, in all likelihood, to push himself, still, it was his decision—to work seventy-seven hours in a row did not help his case, but the kid—and he was the best worker I've seen in a long time, really understood time, and not just timeliness, not just promptness but time is money is time!, working away always as though each and every millisecond could have been his last, which kept him focused, so, so this is no insult at all, not meant to be a heartless slight in any way—he'd had had seizures before. Epilepsy. His mother, too, had them. Epilepsy. Told the company doctor that.

"Now, aw crap, I'm late for a meeting. Claire! Claire! Can you call Jim and tell him to tell Lucas and everybody from Acedico? I'll be in in five.

"Now. Please send me the video before you make it live. I want full access to the tapes and remember, we agreed I'd have full editorial rights, okay?

"Wait. Hold up. We need to make one thing clear. He passed of natural causes, is what I mean to say. Anyway, how I like to think of him: dying doing what he loved best, a kind of prayer thing for him, almost, work. Dying smiling."

A Little
Bank in My Soul

YOU LEFT THE CLOSET LIGHTS ON and a bruised eggplant cut in two on the counter and you left. Other things need to be decided still. The car. I appreciate that you didn't take it and fled by bus instead, but you did pay half and I want to honor that. As we were all expecting—my mom caught a stand-by flight but arrived an hour too late, especially hard since they were estranged—my grandmother passed in Florida two days ago, a place she had never wanted to go, as you know, and neither do I, except that she willed her car to me. I would drive hers back to Milwaukee, then title ours to read your name only, but I have been paying the rent singlehandedly for the past two months. You signed the lease, too, unless you left the line blank while the landlady lorded her gripes over us, droning about the last tenants' children, listing their encyclopedia of noises and offering imitations. I cannot find our copy of the contract so I do not know.

What did you want me to do, babe? Let you run out the door while you yelled down the hallway, swearing over your shoulder that you'd follow the thirty others who've jumped from the Hoan Bridge, that you'd do so without any fanfare, thank you, and faster than I could dial emergency you'd be at the bottom of Lake Michigan, floating up.

Remember how we laughed the first few months, our bedroom right above hers, wondering whether she would tattle to some future tenants, showing and telling the new noises we contributed to her volumes. She did have hearing aids and she said she took them out at night and I thought maybe that was her hint that we need not worry about her overhearing, but as you know I tend to read into these things unduly. Funny how funny things aren't funny now.

Repetition becomes redundancy, the ruin of many good things, but I have to once more say I will never cease to be grateful to you for not having the child. This godawful snap is impossible to endure already and think of all the other things we'd be cutting in half and all the halves we'd have to hold together to keep the child together. And, absent infant or other mortality, this would go on for years, for a lifetime, really—I can't, I couldn't touch it. Without doubt this was the single most selfless thing you did for me and I won't forget that. Never. Though sometimes I—it's just, it seems like an extension of your self-absorption and not the heroic thing you swore it was.

Unfortunately, things as they are still have knots I can't undo alone. Veritable umbilical cords that need cutting before they ring around the neck and choke. Of the rent due next week I am willing to pay up to $800 even. And then there's the snow blower which I was against from the start in spite of my back I swear I would have kept the sidewalks clean just as I had winters prior. Yes, you were right that if someone is going to spend money on a machine like that buying a high-end one makes sense, because everything is built to break now but the gilded ones go a little more slowly. The bottom line is you handed over seven hundred dollars and by all measures the contraption is yours. But if you can't commit to sending at least four hundred a month then you give me no other choice but to sell the thing, which will probably land me $299 at best, based on a quick perusal of the snow blower market. Which means one month where I'm not putting in overtime.

Not that I know what to do with my time. I can't bring myself to go crying to Father Francisco over at Our Lady of Sorrows. At the end of our last meeting, after the baby thing, he hugged me too long. Or maybe it was me, clinging to him. Probably. The point is you don't want to get too close to anyone or anything.

Last night I slept on the floor, which is to say I did not sleep. The couch remains covered in your cat's hair—what did you do with Foster?—and the mold in this place already agitates my allergies. Another discovery: your body must have blocked the draft that comes in from the west window. It creeps up under our feather blanket, feigning weightlessness, whispering up and over me and then suddenly compressive, trying to anchor me down. The price of a broken lease is steep. For now, then, I am sleeping on the floor, which is to say the bed would be all yours if you returned.

Babe, I burned the envelopes I used to load with wrongs and mail away. You are under no obligation to call me but I wanted to ask if you would, because help me see how in hell you don't you lose your mind? I'm still lost in the manuals of moral qualms cooked up by those Jesuits who had me for nearly eighteen years, and you know how hard it is, for novices like me, to let the baby be. If in this interim I can't at least ask you to forgive me I think I'll—not Hoan Bridge, but———————————————————

——————————————————————because by now the restless guilt, nowhere to go, has erected a little bank in my soul. And is gaining interest.

A letter with your latest past due loan balance is enclosed within this envelope.

Sick at the Thought

LITTLE MICHAEL LET HIMSELF IN the backdoor, his skinny hand firm around the hydraulic meant to ease the door shut without slam, his black bangs cut in such a way that the line left there was almost inhuman, a concision that existed only in mathematical ideals. Always precise—an awesome exactitude that defined their whole lives. His parents took that sort of thing very seriously. Little Michael poised between the door and the slam. He would not let it ease shut. He would not have it sound at all. *Come out*, he mouthed without noise. *Come out*, his neck jerking to the side and back.

Billy sat at the green table, his head barely overhanging the surface, chin touching his plate. Billy listened behind to the sound in the bathroom, the hairdryer's hum. It was still on high. It would still be two or three minutes. He gave his friend the look, something between a glare and a dare. The bagel sopped up the whole plate's leftovers. He pressed hard, starting at the center and moving out in circles to sponge clean the gelatinous grape crumbs. The thrill of sweet on his tongue, then the perk of something else, Tabasco maybe—residue of last night's dinner. The plate looked practically unused, and he set a clean fork next to it. Grandma would not settle for dirty dishes on the table, but he could by no means set the thing down in the sink without sound. He thought, something like a prayer, *Please let her come into the kitchen before Mom does, please send me something to stall Mom*. His cheek took the balled-up bagel well, and he fashioned himself a baseball player, minor league at least, chewing. And Little Michael flung the door open wide. A dare. A demand. Billy would have to either exit fast or risk his mother hearing the bang.

"Come on," Little Michael said, when Billy caught up beside him.

"Where are we going?" asked Billy.

"Your mom's getting married," Little Michael said.

"Don't do it," Billy said, "Whatever. Not today," feeling already the itchy pain at the edge of his eyes.

"Seriously. And you're going to have a sibling."

"A what?"

"A sister. Or a brother. You have to be ready."

"I am."

"No you're not."

"For what?"

"I'll show you." Little Michael felt low in the pocket of his thin blue jeans and pulled out a small bullet-shaped container and pointed it at Billy. "Here," he said, leading him around the alleyway to his garage, which was three houses down. The alley was as gray as the smoke that Billy had seen come from his mother's mouth, these days, as he spied through the upper bedroom window, through the folded-over shade that by now stayed that way, folded over, dogeared like the most important page of a book, when she would sit out on the swing in the last reaches of some insomniac streetlight and have her cigarettes. Billy would count them. Seven, sometimes, at a time. In between came the calmest part, when the backyard swing would whine a bit and darkness would cover the earth. Then there would be light again, no larger than the oval of a peach seed, and then gray again. His bare feet freezing on the tiled floor, bent at the toes to see her. Sometimes he cracked the window to hear. Sometimes she said things to herself out loud.

The silver canister, which was no bigger than Little Michael's hand, overflowed with creamed coffee. "I added milk so you wouldn't get sick. I remember the last time I let you try my dad's coffee you got real sick, and got all sad, too, and told your mom. But you're not going to tell your mom anything this time, because I thought it all through. I'm looking after your best interest." He said this last line with a mangled face that made Little Michael look older than his father. "I brought coffee because I need you to be awake. Fully awake. Can you be awake?"

"I am awake," Billy said, fingering the nose-rest of his thick brown glasses.

"My dad says we need to be vigilant, which means *wide awake*. He says the President sent him a signed paper calling on people such as himself to be awake. Things are falling apart in this country. My dad's the one who told me that your mom is getting married. And he's the one who told my mom that it wasn't going to last. I wasn't supposed to hear that but. Look, I thought I'd tell you now so you're *vigilant* when the man starts living in your house and all that.

"My dad knows the President, so he knows things. I wouldn't trouble you if he didn't. Some of my friends' dads think they know things, but they don't. My dad told me that too. Look. I have been given directions by him because *he knows*. I am to find the mail stack at any new friend's house. There I am to look for letters reading *MILL COUNTY HUMAN SERVICES*. If I see an envelope that reads that way I am still to be friends with the boy, but I am to understand that his parents are in need of my exemplary behavior, really, because they are in the same position as me. Do you know what exemplary means? Good. I thought you would, even though you're younger than me. You have a good head on your shoulders. My dad said that. Anyhow, my point is that I'm a *dependent*. I can't provide for myself. And neither can they. So we're both at the same level. But I'm *supposed* to be a dependent, whereas they're supposed to be holding their own by now but they can't help being babied. He said I can make up my own mind if I want to feel bad for them or not. Geezeus. My dad's real smart. He's out of town on business, but he calls every night. My mom and I wait by the phone around eight o'clock and he always calls. He's real responsible."

Billy was rubbing at a spot of coffee that was bleeding outward from where it dripped and burned by his crotch. The blue jeans had darkened there to almost black. His hair was laid densely around his head, hay-colored like roofs in certain northern Wisconsin towns, falling down around his forehead in a mussed way. Some of the houses even had ewes eating at the green grass. Billy gulped a good measure of coffee, loudly so that there would be no questions. He would not get sick again.

Thin stretches of tar like serpents cooked in the sun and now dead covered the cracks of the gray alleyway.

"Someday soon we'll be out of this neighborhood," Little Michael said, his eyes fixed on the tar, the three basketball backboards without rims, the red and green innards of the exposed powerline swinging down from the sky. "This was my grandparents' neighborhood, my parents' parents' house. Things were good then here. Now anyone can live here. People can save up money because they don't have to pay for their own food because half the city is on foodstamps. So now you have all kinds here. My parents talk about moving a lot. After he comes back from this trip they're putting up our house for sale. Between you and me. This is why I need to talk with you now. Because you need to be ready for things. Otherwise you might run away. You can't run away." Billy rubbed his eyes. They were flitting now and he could not hold his concentration in one place for more than a few seconds. He finally focused on the exposed wire, above the garage. He shivered as though the thing had just finished touching his shoulder. It hung down like a thin hand beckoning him he knew not where. Away.

Little Michael was satisfied enough. He started down the side of the baby blue garage, looked meanly through the fence toward the back bay window of his parents' kitchen, and turned the golden handle of the garage door.

A weak breath of light covered most of the empty inside with blue-gray. The sides were still dark, shadows. Little Michael disappeared there for a while, pulled back what sounded like the sack used to cover the mower. Then came a wobbly, bouncy sound. He appeared, his face a smudge of sweaty peach sucking quick breaths. He called Billy over to him with a wink, the clasping of his single eyelid barely visible in the cobalt shade. But his eyes were somehow yellow. Not ominous like a cat's. Sickly almost for the first time. He was always the healthiest. Billy obeyed, and Little Michael motioned him to sit down. They were both on the ground now, and both could see enough to know that their pants would be soiled with the island of oil they now sat upon. The concrete was cold.

"Here it is," Little Michael said, and he unfolded the wobbly, twanging pages, bending the backbone of the magazine so that only one image could be seen. Billy squinted, squeezed some vision from the greedy dim. He saw first a pale pear, upside down. The color of a pear picked before season. But his mouth objected. It was wet. Not with bile. He would not get sick.

"I caught my dad with these last year. He was in the bathroom, in the middle of the night, when I went in to pee. His face went very far away and then he said, 'It's nothing! Out! I'm getting ready for it. Your mother.' He didn't mean to talk. I had caught him off guard. He's only human, see. Even though he's very responsible. The magazine was laid out across the sink. Two naked women arranged in these strange poses. In one a man stood over her. 'This is not for your mother to know,' he said. 'She has enough trouble right now.' He'd pulled up his underwear by then. My mom called to him from the bedroom. I couldn't sleep for hours. I pretended like I was walking back to bed, all the way down the other end of the house. I turned back in about five minutes. I thought I heard a dog. You know the way that old lady's dog gets, down the street, snarling and sticking its face in the dirt. I heard that sound come from the bedroom.

"I asked my dad about it the next day. He said it was nothing to be afraid of, the noise. But he was sorry we had had to meet the way we did, in the bathroom. But he said something in him told him it was alright. It was not ideal timing, but it was something I should know. My dad is real honest. Other people would try to hide it, he said."

Billy's eyes absorbed what had previously been an upside down pear. It was now the butt of a woman, bent toward his face. He felt something like a rash run across his cheeks.

"You have to be ready for these things. That new man's gonna come into your house and you're gonna hear these sounds. But it's okay. Even if it sounds like a mean dog. You can't look at it like that. It's okay."

Then the side door swung open and a rectangular slab of light about the size of a prominent gravestone fell upon them both. They bent a bit under its weight. Billy saw Little Michael's hands try to move. They tried to fold the glossy, durable page inward, then pulled at the edges as though to rip it in half. Nothing worked. His mother was there, her long red-brown hair tied up around her head, sprays of strands hanging down, the bleak light coloring it beautifully. Like water made of fire. Falling down from her head, falling down around her reddening temples.

Two days later she wrote Billy's mother a letter. Little Michael, sneaking to the door in the twilight, told Billy that his mother told him not to tell his father. Not any of it. It would be too much for him, she said. He was busy enough and stressed enough as it was. The letter was written on the inside of a sympathy card. The card's cover had a bouquet of sunflowers on the front, some of their black seeds shown in the motion of falling down to the ground. It read:

> Dear Neighbor,
>
> We are so sorry for your loss. It is a humbling thing to have something like this get out. We are sure you will not share it with too many others. I am sure Billy told you everything. I am sick at the thought. I am so sorry for your loss. For what you have lost. If you believe in forgiveness, mercy, what have you. If you could, try.
>
> > Grieving with you,
> > Jacklyn and Ed

She had signed for both of them.

Billy had told his mother none of it. The letter opened his mouth so that everything came out. It took him an hour to say it in a way that made any sense. What he had lost. Then he knew what he had lost. As best he could. His birthday party was forty-five minutes away when they finished talking, mother and child. His uncle was coming. A professional clown. He and his mother spent their remaining time alone on their knees.

"Kneel down here," she said, half pulling him over to the base of the couch. Grandpa slept through everything, a partially eaten hardboiled egg laid across his lap on a tissue. "Dear God," she said, "Wash his mind." She said so many other things and Billy was amazed at how familiar God was to her.

Then they were on their knees again, scrubbing the kitchen floor with water that reeked of lime, ginger, and bleach. They had gloves on their hands when Little Michael came for the party. He was the first guest. Billy's mother checked the clock with the rooster on the end of its long hand. Ten minutes early. They couldn't give him a proper welcome because they had gloves on their hands and the gloves had dangerous chemicals on them. She tried to say this with a smile. Spit came out when she spoke. Some of it struck Little Michael. Her son was turning nine today.

That time. Those times.

Once, a year later, the police came personally to escort Little Michael's father to what must have been one of the most important events of his life.

"Probably he's going to see the President," Billy said, his nose and lips against the big bay window, the clean-looking father of his best friend a giant, so tall, bending hard as an officer helped him lower his neck and take the back seat. The way a chauffeur helps a client settle into the irresponsibility of the rear.

Thomas, the man who asked him daily to call him *Dad*, neither nodded nor said no. He ran his fingers along the poorly-tuned piano, lightly so as not to wake Grandpa, who snored vigilantly in the large, brown leather recliner, his brittle body fattened by two long underwear shirts, hidden under two checkered blankets, one black and gray, and one black and blue.

The next morning when Billy sifted through the sprawled newspapers in search of the comics he saw that one of the cartoon cat's heads had been blotted out by a black permanent marker. He traced the blotch back to its origins several pages away, an article with much underlining, several lines even, in some places, enunciating the words TOO BIG TO FAIL and SLAP ON THE WRIST. There was a picture of a tall man, a giant really. It was the back of his head as he bent into a limousine. A man with a gnarled nose that stuck out between wiry glasses blocked the giant's face. The blocker's teeth were frozen in a gnashed position. The eyes were drawn more there than to the man hiding behind him, half gone.

Later, many years later, Thomas told him the whole thing as the two painted a high rise one summer. The police sirens had drawn them all from their settled routine, from the things they did every night while mom worked second shift at the emergency clinic. After Thomas returned everything to its place, righting that routine by wrapping Billy beneath the thick quilted blanket that always smelled of Grandpa's rum cigarillo smoke no matter how many times it was washed, the man he was told now to call Dad slipped out the door like a man involved in an affair, holding the hydraulic so that he wouldn't even leave a soft sound in his wake, and knocked on Little Michael's door.

When no one answered he tiptoed around the back, felt the door handle to see if it turned, and let his feet work their way in and walk him through the path lit by cottony lights that gleamed behind papery white circles placed everywhere. Chinese lanterns. No plain bulbs here.

Little Michael let out loud rhythmic exhales from his little bedroom, but these could only be discerned if one adjusted to the machine next to his bed. The machine released the sound of a seashore. Waves, without the scent of the sea, beating against the walls of the gray machine, spilling through its speakers. Seagulls crying here and there. It was meant to keep things calm.

Thomas found her in the subdued scarlet light of the bathroom. Little Michael's mother. Her flushed cheek rested against the toilet bowl. Her carefully pressed hair, its red-orange fire still raining in gorgeous strands from her skull, was drawn back so that it stayed out of the yellow-blue mess that filled the toilet.

Pulled back, a layer of gray showed underneath. Her mouth chewed slowly and her eyes were occupied with some vision that prevented her from reacting to Thomas.

"What can I do?" he asked.

She spat out the mashed pixels of what had been airbrushed breasts, thighs, legs, and this was followed by a deeper heave which gripped her bowels and brought up more bile. She was eating the other women one by one, regurgitating their picturesque flesh, her body rejecting their inky blood, their unleavened waists. *Have me, have all of me for free*, they said in so many words. Thomas did not hear them, but she did and this is what they said. She told him.

"Call the doctor," she said, then, leaning heavy on the toilet.

"911?" Thomas asked. "What should I say?"

"Tell them I'm dying. A woman is dying or her mind at least is for Christ's sake call the doctor."

"Okay," he said. "We'll have Michael over for a sleep over. I'll see if I can't carry him over without him even waking up. Do you have any blankets? I'll call the doctor but I just—we'll take him for the night. No problem."

"You can't do that. He'll wake up most definitely," she said. "He would wake up and then—. Are you crazy?"

The paramedics measured her pulse. She persuaded them to put her in the back of the ambulance and the orderly complied. He had become more amicable after laughing, still maintaining some semblance of the professional poker face but laughing knowingly nonetheless, before both her and Thomas. And then he said, "Alright, we'll take you in," as though he was paying her back for the chance to chortle out a little condescension. Thomas said to her, when they had a moment alone: "They don't pay these ambulance drivers much. Minimum wage at best."

She was shuffled from the emergency room to the psychiatric ward. There were many people in the waiting room whose way was paid for by the Human Services. Little Michael's mother looked at them longingly, as though she wanted to be them or was them or what she did not know. She picked up a magazine. It had taken two treatments to get all the pictures up from out of her belly. They had washed her tongue of the black and blue blood of the ink. Here, in the waiting room, the women were not quite nude, in the magazines. She did not feel the need to shred them.

The psychiatrist called her in. He listened for a long time, here and there lifting a metal ball that fell and clanked a series of other metal balls. Listened to her whole life. Then tried the following technique:

"It is only ink," he said. "You can't look at it as though he was with other women. That isn't helpful. We need to think of what will be helpful right now. What will replace the—this difficult thing, and put something manageable in its place. It is only ink. Two dimensional ink. Not people. Not real women. Don't think too much about it. Just think that it is only ink, if that is helpful. If not try something else. Millions of men do the same…" he trailed off as a spray of blue cleanser pummeled the windows' outside.

Thomas tried to put his arm around her shoulder. She had told the psychiatrist he was her brother. She needed to lean on him to walk from room to room. As though they were alone, as though the psychiatrist wasn't waiting like a delivery doctor for whatever she could push out, Little Michael's mother told Thomas little jokes about the doctor prescribing his own medicine, therefore the cheer. A man, suspended some seven stories above the earth, hovered over them, running a rubber squeegee over the glass. The student intern who sat across the room, on a small sofa, studied the psychiatrist. Her hand scrawled hard words onto a pale yellow pad. He started again, his voice less certain this time: "The thing is, you need to do what works for you, what will be most helpful for you to overcome… to really reckon with the ambiguity that is really, I mean, a *part* of life, it's, it's hard to come to that conclusion, I know. But it's—if I can use the word—true." Little Michael's mother watched her hand reach out and strike him, saw a little leak of red where the diamond of her ring had scratched the thick glasses lens that protected his eye. The student intern stood up to get help. Help.

The Dead Letter Office

To Whom It May Concern,

We regret to inform you that your father died in the early hours on January 1.

Death. 1. The termination of life. The expiration of life. The end of life. (*These conventional definitions of death are, finally, contingent upon the definition of life. There is no consensus concerning the definition of life.*) 2. The definitive and undying termination of all bodily processes essential to vitality. (*There is no consensus concerning the definition of vitality, nor any authoritative explanation of essentiality.*) 3. Common law considers death "an absence of spontaneous respiratory and cardiac functions." (*There is no consensus concerning "absence," especially as absence can in a certain sense increase presence, as in the saying "absence makes the heart grow fonder."*)

We recommend that you think of the aforementioned definitions of death as a multiple choice test in which there is no wrong answer. The difficulty with there being no wrong answer is that there is also no right answer. Please do not cry. Although the common law bids us inform you of your father's death, you are free to disagree with each of the above definitions, because what "life" means is for each person to determine. There is no consensus. You will understand, then, that whereas good manners would have us send our sympathies and condolences, doing so would be to manipulate you into the assumption that your father has really and truly and actually died in a manner that implies disadvantageous loss and thus prescribes mourning. Think of it this way: your father *may* have been (please note the emphasis on *may*, an accentuation of possibility as opposed to certainty) no more than a collection of perceptions and feelings and disparate deeds. He may have been nothing more than the convenient reduction of an overwhelming multiplicity to a single individual (or alternately a person, a self, etc.). Identity may well be a synonym for despair. It would appear that the same holds for the rest of us.

Some of the most successful recipients of our notifications have recognized it as equally plausible that the atoms which were previously trapped into the configuration of a single mind-body form are now free to scatter with great vitality to the ends of the earth and even, with some luck, beyond the boundaries of the demarcated cosmos. But, again, life and death are ultimately a matter of personal preference. Some of us are not so adventurous. Confronted with the apparent termination of what we have grown accustomed to calling "life," "vitality," "cardiac function," others find solace in shouting an earsplitting dirge that climaxes in *Aiee! Aieeeeee!*, accompanied by some variation of shattered glass, slammed doors that unhinge from their jambs, potshards scraped against the skin, followed by squatting in sackcloth, staring judiciously at the scattered ashes saying "The Lord gave, and the Lord has taken away."

Best wishes,
All of Us at The Dead Letter Office

Darkly I Gaze
into the Days Ahead

With your mercury mouth in the missionary times,
And your eyes like smoke and your prayers like rhymes,
And your silver cross, and your voice like chimes,
Who do they think could bury you?
With your pockets well protected at last,
And your streetcar visions which you place on the grass,
And your flesh like silk, and your face like glass,
Who could they get to carry you?

Sad-eyed lady of the lowlands,
Where the sad-eyed prophet says that no man comes,
My warehouse eyes, my Arabian drums,
Should I put them by your gate,
Or, sad-eyed lady, should I wait?
                —Bob Dylan, "Sad-Eyed Lady of the Lowlands"

WHEN Sister Maria Josepha of the Child Jesus founded Mater
Dei High School seventy seven years earlier, she had the novices
carve into woodcuts the designs of the Miraculous Medal: M-
shaped hills crowned with the cross and encircled by an ovular
run of stars. To the newly-professed whose hands had more
finesse, she assigned the medal's other side. Into treated cherry
they chiseled the veiled woman whose surrendered hands emitted little lines of light. For days all the nuns dipped these images
into donated trays of azure paint and pressed them surreptitiously to the milky borders of every room in the building.

This morning, in a world that seemed planets away from that one, Mr. Ellison nonetheless found himself petitioning the faded blue Mother of God whose eyes remained perpetually wide. Hers did not itch at the paralyzed motes, trapped and ancient dust that made the room permanently musty. The students, too, seemed sickened by the particularly stale air, most of them slumped, hands slack at their sides.

Enough. Repeating the line *Darkly I gaze into the days ahead* three times, he spun his wheelchair and coaxed it to the desk. Lifting a rusted scissors from the screeching drawer, he rolled toward the window, his reddened eyes vacillating between students surrendered to sleep and Mary's outstretched arms until the two became one inside the stars that studded the medal's circumference. He gnawed the blade into the thick paint that sealed the window shut and then shoved it upward only to find it fall again and nearly crush his fingers. Reaching into the frame, he pulled at the sash stuck at the base. Tugging too hard, he snapped free the cast iron weight. The window rose and a rush of chilled air sent the students up straight. Dangling the rusted brown iron from the sash, Ellison recited the rest:

> And little lads, lynchers that were to be,
> Danced round the dreadful thing in fiendish glee.

He said the words *lads* and *lynchers* with a softness that made the class have to strain to hear.

Twenty eight terrified pairs of eyes studied the verse and the weight that dangled there. Having won their attention at last, ready to get lost in his Harlem Renaissance lecture, the unerring hands of time pointed a damning finger. Late. Ellison, who wore the same baby blue suit every day, glided to the doorway and, descending the disability ramp, guided his class in a gangling, zigzagging line, looking over his shoulder and hollering at the stragglers: "If a cripple can beat you to the gym, you got real troubles, kids!" As the class approached the newly-waxed, state-of-the-art gymnasium, he flicked the dandruff from his shoulders, patted the edges of his natty hair and exhaled loudly, the sound circling back into his ears and drowning out the furor gathering inside.

When his students entered the gym one of the cafeteria ladies—a smiling, starved-looking woman who always ladled out the mush with a nervous twitch—handed each student a miniature American flag, a bobblehead effigy of the presidential candidate, and blue T-shirts that said *Be Bold Witz, Get us off the Dole Witz!* on the front and on the reverse. All of the other classes already filled the wooden bleachers, choreographed carefully according to color-coded shirts, so that their very bodies spelled out WITZBOLD FOR PRESIDENT in white, the name floating on a sea of blue, the edges of the letters roughened when students squirmed. The candidate, who had donated millions to develop the school's sports facilities, was an alumnus of Mater Dei High, once a prestigious and now a charter school smack in the center of the gutted, dilapidated, but still populous center of the city.

Through fanfare of kazoos and balloons, just under a Witzbold blimp that levitated precariously above the crowd, Ellison saw his student Devin, who was all slunk reluctance, jerk his bicep back and nearly rub noses with a man in all black whose back said SERVE-U-STAFF. The man in black gripped the bicep tighter and half flung Devin toward his classmates as they ascended the bleachers to assume their assigned seating. SERVE-U-STAFF followed suit, his finger on Devin's neck, but he let go of the young man and scaled down the steep steps when he made eye contact with a camera leering down from on high. STAFF's hands fell into his pockets and his chin dropped to the nape of his neck as he became conscious of the omnipresent surveillance—the gym covered by a few film crews' worth of cameras, microphones, mixing boards and wires, all of this guarded by a woman who wore a *Don't Tread on Me* T-shirt under her snakeskin blazer.

The principal met Ellison at the base of the stands just as the STAFF man shoved Devin up, his hand outstretched in a manner that mimicked almost perfectly the presidential candidate's own high-profile conciliatory gesture. When the principal saw the shove up above, and saw that Ellison saw, he put his free arm around the young teacher's back and hugged him with a pivot that eliminated the scene from even their periphery. Over the marching band's staccato punches the principal said "Don't let your politics get in the way, Theodore," meant for no one else's ears but said loudly by necessity on account of the clamor. And Ellison, straight-faced and somber, responded, "I hope you said the same thing to Mr. Witzbold," before he marched the rest of his class to the only place that remained, a stripe of stained oak benches just behind the center of the suddenly-muted pandemonium. Ellison searched the bleachers frantically, hoping to find any other openings, at the base but further away. Nothing. This was it. Gingerly, Ellison half-stood and half-fell back onto a patch of bleacher, nearly sitting on a student who smelled of marijuana, motionless eyes hypnotized by the unfurled flags and phantasmagoric lights.

Ellison was trapped—crushed, actually. The kid must have eaten many bags of the potato chips he now slipped from his pocket and poured into his mouth before, turning to Ellison as to a peer, he offered the remnant crumbs. On Ellison's other side—the same proximity as that of a catcher waiting behind the batter—a thin rectangular speaker delivered mythic thunder as the candidate materialized onstage, his maroon, pointed-toe dress shoes clomping in congruence with the crowd's clapping.

Except for the pockets of saggy flesh which guarded his eyes, the candidate's skin was tanned orange, and his dyed blonde hair looked, one smart aleck news anchor had quipped, "like the standard Cancun wig for old men just vain enough to primp their looks." The candidate's bulk had been thinned by the masterful art of his seamstress, but Witzbold still hefted his weight as he approached the microphone stand. The high school's cheerleaders, clad in martyr's red and the blue of shining seas, jumped rope and clapped palms to the refrain and antiphon:

> We don't want
> *Handouts*
> We don't want
> *Handouts*
> Won't live and die for these
> *Handouts*
> Won't live and die for these
> *Handouts*

Witzbold clapped his hands—tanned on the outside but palms as pale as a funeral pall—fixing pleased eyes on the twirling rope. Its sustained movement formed the shape of a single, massive eye, until the cheerleaders wound down the routine and retreated to their bench. The candidate's eyes followed their thighs until, like a child at a zoo, his attention was arrested by a baby elephant. An outsourced tamer led the animal, but atop it, waiving and grinning with finesse, rode this year's prom queen. Her body, like the elephant's, was blue above the waist and red beneath. The same paint covered woman and beast. Ellison sat on his fisted hands. Her black hair had been dyed blonde, but strands of dark counterpointed the bleachy yellow. As the elephant skulked across the center of the gym, the prom queen rose and blew a kiss to the candidate. After she scrunched her lip her body seemed to lapse into a mannequin condition. Her hands held tight. When she shut her eyes the stars painted over them became brighter. At a signal from the tamer the animal turned toward the stage and all eyes saw a golden microphone curled in its trunk. The creature extended it to the candidate, who at once looked as if he had returned from a week spent receiving massages and eating.

As the elephant and the rider departed, he tapped the microphone and said, "My fellow Americans. Let's not allow politics to put us at odds with one another. Join me, if you will, by doing something that unites us all." He raised his right hand as though to wave but then turned it back on himself and let it rest just above his heart. Then, sweet blue eyes squinting soberly at the flag that spanned almost an entire gym wall, he pledged allegiance.

But Mr. Ellison did not rise with the rest. Could not. Cajoling his contorted hand over his left breast, Ellison let his tongue hinge on the rails of the old familiar words. His vacant eyes kept opaque the thoughts that thumped through his mind, elephantine. *Where're we at? The politician's promising not to get political.*

Poised behind the podium, his magnified voice orchestrating the several hundred students and their teachers, Witzbold slowed and intoned the final words: *one nation indivisible, under God.* Witzbold scratched just below his eye at the word *one,* and, turning slightly to avoid the light that tormented his eyes, he pivoted an inch to the left and caught Ellison in his peripheral.

Witzbold's distorted grimace—formed by lips curled well into the mouth and clamped firmly by unseen teeth—made Ellison's right leg kick, as when a doctor tests the reflexes. But, remembering the holes in the bottom of his shoe, he squeaked his feet back into place. He tried but failed to pull his body inward, holding his breath as though he could thin himself to the point of invisibility. For a few seconds he thought he had succeeded, as Witzbold was searching elsewhere. But then Witzbold was jerking a thumb toward him, facing the crowd and mouthing *Booooooo*. The concentration of hundreds of eyes and cameras remained on Ellison's crooked frame as Witzbold descended the stage. With noble steps, he shook a row of freshman hands, making his way towards Ellison, whose hips started to sweat. The presidential candidate made clear his intention.

"Two things I love about America," he said. "The self-determination to select your own destiny, to make yourself whatever you want, a thing, a great thing, the greatest which we all know and love, and see here today in a private school made possible by the tax dollars of students whose parents and guardians have chosen to send them *here* rather than *there*"—and at "there" he shot a sore thumb motion over his shoulder, at the city's rotted core. "Number two. The right of all Americans to *prefer not to*. Mr." he said, lowering his microphone to "Ellison," whose Adam's apple rose and fell like the jackhammers going strong outside. "Mr. Ellison," Witzbold continued, "has a *right* not to pledge allegiance to the United States of America, just as *we* the people have a *right* to—come on everybody—say *Booooo*. C'mon, let me hear you!"

A smattering of souls replied, but the sound came out *Whooooooo?*

"Now, I'm not sure of Mr. Ellison's particular *motives* behind his preferring *not to*," he said, looking at Ellison as though the teacher were a show contestant who, fresh from the green room, had just been schooled in the etiquette expected of him, but who ignored even the easiest dictates of entertainment.

"I didn't," Ellison said. "I'm *not* preferring not—," he went on, gesturing with scrawny, crippled fingers, some still white with fresh chalk. Against his will, the hand battered his heart three times, the dreaded motion that randomly overcame him.

Witzbold imitated him, whapping a fat hand against his chest.

His lips loosened and the left side of his face lifted in a toothy smile. A piece of paper fell, sweat-whetted, fell from Ellison's hand. The lint-dusted thing landed in his lap. Witzbold lunged forward and, like a raffle caller reaching into the bowl, he closed his eyes until his pincers plucked the well-worn page. Peeling it apart at the heavy creases, his auctioneer voice assuming a low bellow tone, the words he read slipped through his throat like a neck through a noose:

> *His spirit is smoke ascended to high heaven.*
> *His father, by the cruelest way of pain,*
> *Had bidden him to his bosom once again;*
> *The awful sin remained still unforgiven.*
> *All night a bright and solitary star*
> *(Perchance the one that ever guided him,*
> *Yet gave him up at last to Fate's wild whim)*
> *Hung pitifully o'er the swinging char.*
> *Day dawned, and soon the mixed crowds came to view*
> *The ghastly body swaying in the sun:*
> *The women thronged to look, but never a one*
> *Showed sorrow in her eyes of steely blue;*
> *And little lads, lynchers that were to be,*
> *Danced round the dreadful thing in fiendish glee.*

Witzbold elevated the piece of paper, waving it like a white flag, as if to emphasize that the words were not his own. "Claude McKay," he finished.

While Witzbold read, Ellison felt like an accused, as though an incompetent authority was conducting a public strip search, spilling and spelling out his secrets, and, as the poem went on, as though the speaker was slicing a little slit into his side, siphoning out his central nervous system, shaking it out like a drenched string, and then returning it with a guilty look that said, "Good as New!"

Then Ellison entered a new smallness that he had never known before, a smallness not undesirable or oppressive. As he stared longer at the presidential candidate, the freckles became little faces, faces and faces of citizens, until Witzbold's whole body was nothing but a multitude, held-together who knew how.

"You're—" Witzbold said. *Retard,* he nearly mouthed before he caught himself and, backing away, ascended the stage steps, "Are we alright, everybody? It's getting kind of *stuffy* in here. Too serious. Way too serious. Politics is supposed to be fun, am I right?"

The audience valved out a submissive applause. When the candidate paced from side to side along the stage edge, nearly teetering in his task to milk more noise, the claps rose a decibel.

"I'm sympathetic to what this McKay's saying. Trust me. I love poetry. Really. I think the real heart of what he's saying and you're saying with your little protest here is that the absolute power corrupts absolutely and, believe me, do I know it! You wanna know who has the absolute power right now? It's not the politicians! It's the press!"

Witzbold grinned, watching the accused with a belly full of worry. Glancing down at a small off-white square of notes he had tucked up his sleeve, he hunted for the right words. A rogue cameraman followed his gaze, honed in on *I love black people* and, though the candidate's thumb obscured the next few bullet points, the picture captured the final line: *You've always been the backbone of the nation.*

Witzbold lifted the microphone like a mover of marionettes. "Bring back the elephant!" he cried. And the animal materialized at once, its back burdened by no rider. Wrapping the rope around her wrists, the tamer, whose hair matched the color of the creature she had trained, told the elephant to spin in a circle. All the while an outer rung of cheerleaders tossed flaming golden torches to the heavens and caught them with poise. Witzbold orchestrated those closest to him, who had formed and now sustained the pyramidal eye of a dollar bill. He joined in as they sang a grand finale of:

> We don't want
> *Handouts*
> We don't want
> *Handouts*
> Don't make us live for these
> *Handouts*
> Don't make us die for these
> *Handouts*
> Be be be bold, Witz!
> *Get us off the Dole, Witz*
> Be be be bold, Witz!
> *Get us off the Dole, Witz*

And then Witzbold, straining to recall what was supposed to happen next, turned pale, as though a funeral march was tromping his brain. He bit his lip and buried the script. He folded his hands together like a trunk, swinging them toward the tamer, saying, "Bring that thing over here, would ya?" Barely heaving himself up the elephant's side, he mounted the saddle. Astride the mascot, he waved and winked and pointed, swaying precariously back and forth. At first he shook like a child whose training wheels have been weaned, and young terror appeared on his face. But the shock wore off as he let the contagious applause and the raucous laughter of the crowd cover over everything, entertaining away the void, that annoyance that threatened whenever the constant stream of twittering dins ceased.

Later, from the remote-controlled bed of a recovery room suite at Our Lady of the Seven Dolors Hospital, Witzbold watched it all happen again. As soon as he woke, still seeing black when he blinked, still comfortably numbed by the IV painkillers, his wife spooning his favorite brand of sweet tapioca into his sour face, Witz called his media man and had him purchase every single tape—every noise and every picture and every last little clip—recorded that day. *Threats if necessary. Money no limit.* After bargaining with the nurse, he managed to pack an entire production crew and all of their equipment into his room. Seven expert editors appeared within hours, including a master from Hollywood. When he grew tired of the arm sling and the leg cast, he had his wife give him oxycodone from a little metal case, shaped like a pyx, in her purse. A large *W* puffed out from the case's cover, as though its ballooned type swelled with helium. Witzbold ignored the knockings of doctors and aides, remaking the day that launched his campaign. He remained hard at work, directing and delegating, like a doctor at a dying man's bedside. As the night wore into morning and the second dose of oxycodone toured his veins, the candidate swore more and elbowed away all expert advice.

And then he leaked it all to the press.

Mr. Ellison arrived at the faculty lounge early in order to read the free copy of *State of the Nation.* The night had been nothing but turning like raw meat on a rotisserie spit, twisting over a burning fire. The principal had called him many times before he had finally answered around midnight. He could work for two more weeks and then they would replace him with any number from the "binder of extraordinarily talented candidates who would do anything to have your job."

Ellison's tongue crippled, writhed weakly before it went flaccid. He could not wring an explanation from the limp instrument. He could not counter the confusion, miscommunication.

He shook and he shook. His wrist battered his shoulder blade. He stayed silent until the dial tone droned.

This morning, looking both ways before tucking the newspaper under his wheelchair, Ellison retreated into his homeroom. There, he retrieved the rusted scissors and some aged scotch tape from his drawer. He had seen it all broadcast earlier, just after dawn. The doctored tapes of yesterday. He made gentle cuts around the newspaper's "Entertainment" heading, then stretched it above the headline that read *Witzbold's Miraculous Rise,* covering the bolded word "Politics" with the still-bolder "Entertainment." His moist brown eyes blinked as he looked again at the page. Three stout color photographs crowded the slender text. The columns of words hugged the gutters as though hip-shoved there, cowering, insignificant next to the visions. The candidate and the prom queen riding an elephant. The candidate among the people, his arm around an invisible man who yesterday was Ellison but was now mere absence, edited out entirely. The candidate, like a competitor claiming victory, boasting a Miraculous Medal. The principal, Ellison presumed, must have planned to bestow this honorary emblem upon the school's visitor before the man fell from the elephant. He could still hear the sound of uncensored adolescents lost in riotous appreciation. In the picture, Witzbold palmed the medal with his pale hand. On the medal, which dangled from an Olympian ribbon of red, white, and blue, the oval of stars looked more like a horseshoe, and Witzbold looked more like a boxer gloating over his good luck than a candidate announcing his campaign.

Muttering laughs under his breath, Mr. Ellison made copies and distributed the "Entertainment" section article, straight faced, to his homeroom students. None of them caught his cleverness. None noticed the section switch. Not a one laughed at his joke.

And then the very feet of his being descended a dolorous staircase when, weaving between the rows of desks, he saw that something had gone wrong. A printer error. The Miraculous Medal came out in two different ways. Some of the copies showed the horseshoe of stars, Mary making a speculator's wink. In others, though, Mary winced as the candidate held her high like a trophy, convinced that he and she had just struck an unbelievable deal. Her sad eyes gazed into the lowlands, straining and squinting as they followed the fast-descending valley that dipped between the dramatic spires that punctured the city skyline and needled the cumulonimbus clouds, drawing down raindrops from heaven.

Tears in Things

This is a Hieronymus Bosch of facts and figures
and blood and graphs.
This is a nightmare of narrative slop.
—Lorrie Moore, "People Like That Are the Only People Here"

DEEP BUREAU DRAWERS where no light deposits. Tiptoed, Christine snapped her elbow bone in place, then stretched her straightened arm until it ached. Still, she could not reach the farthest files, the ones with tears in them.

For the last four months, her days had been one long ovary-shaped pace around the apartment, impossible to quiet the twins' cries, Francisco louder and less consolable than Lúcia no matter which of Grandma's remedies she tried: rubbing valerian into coconut oil and massaging this into the abdomen, she sighed; inhaling the basil-steam, too, as she boiled it over the stove, sucking it in herself before she spooned it through his shut lips; she tried warm compresses of lemon balm, fennel and orange blossom and yes she had tried, and tried, and, more than tired in the tedious night, had popped out of joint the arm that rocked and sought to soothe the sweet son, the skinny one who came out scowling under a shock of schist-black hair that spoke the name of his father, Santiago, who slept better than she. Where he was stationed, these days, only the silence sometimes chilled the soldiers awake, camouflage blankets failing them in the long Afghan nights.

Christine had been back at work for a week and now this thankless task. She'd been asked, told, cajoled into doing it by the same priest who, just days after her own mother birthed her, rang the bell with his chin and stepped right in, interrupting her mother's own pacing and presenting a cake as large as the newborn and molded in the shape of a little lamb, complete with calligraphic frosting. *Little Lamb Who Made Thee? Gave thee life and bid thee feed*, which came off as both sweet and creepy simultaneously when her own mother first told her the story, over extortionate margaritas. Christine was sixteen. Mother told it as though she were confessing a crime, for some reason, not just dabbing away the wet rivulets of mascara but continuously reapplying her makeup, so that though she was talking to her daughter she was looking at herself nearly the whole time, staring at the magnified obsidian eyes that the circular compact mirror shot back at her in the clean, well-lit corner booth of La Fuentes, her cousin Hector's restaurant. "Without Father we wouldn't be here," her mother had explained, more than a mist of mystery surrounding her confession. La Fuentes was famous for its overpriced margaritas: you could complain about the cost but you would return again to nurse and then sip and then drain the precious strawberry slush.

When at last, still on tiptoes, Christine could feel the untouchable files, still her fingers could not pinch and pluck them out. Forbidden. The key! Idiot. She'd dangled its ring around her pinky finger, rung it there so as to remember, and had forgotten. The keyring slipped off, seemingly safe in the swallow of a half-gaping folder, but then came the metal clang on the marble floor below. Whatever. Nevermind. Key to nothing soon. Emptied drawers of carefully-sorted nothing. Soon. But now the accordion slots were stuffed with smoothed and flattened testimonies, memos and rehabilitations and reassignments, some folders swelling threateningly—ready to detonate or worse.

Outside a short shatter, followed by a faint scream. Then a voice that might have been talking to her directly, from six feet under where she stood. "Gotdamn, man, I'll kill you." Even in the middle of the night the constant sounds of the city. The weird way that sirens came out as soothes in the wake of a fight. The crescendo and fade of surging cars, she could see them now, half of them without license plates, some of the chassis catching chunks of snow and scraping them along the salted streets, hardened ice clinging like refugees holding on at any cost—nothing to return to, going anywhere.

Salt on the margarita rim, melting her mother's ice chunk edges. Confessions coming out slushed. "Without Father we wouldn't be here." Salt on the streets. Salt of the earth.

Slow motion. Bleary-eyed, beyond tired, staring at the black filing cabinet. Father paid for a nanny, increased her salary, and here she was alone in a little tucked-away room, a forgotten corner the bishop's cook once kept. Blinking siren lights dulled when they passed through the windows' gray-grime, beams unable to permeate the bureau. The old stove's smoke stains kept things well-hid. She scraped two circles, pressed her eyes against the frozen glass. Narrowed her eyes to see. A body struck by a lackluster streetlamp, head slunk. As though the architect had been playing hangman when he made it. Below the lamp a splayed body knocked down, hands holding head—insane snow angel. A woman with a tower of braided hair circled the dead, flailing fingers both begging and condemning, yelling into a cell phone. Christine stifled a sneeze, shook her head like a mother who can't bring herself to scold, yet again, the offense so tediously repeated. The sight so familiar in her neighborhood: hurt and tired and more than tried bodies bent on the sidelines of what we call living.

Christine went back to pulling files, stacking them in two piles. Straight as she had made them, the columns had started to sway. She scraped out a stack of strip club receipts that had fled its proper folder. *Sick ticks.* That's what the bishop had called them. *Sick ticks. Sad S.O.B.s.* Every drawer was stuffed with well-thumbed folders, whose evergreen had not faded yet. Licked thumbs, maybe, had whetted some of the pages' edges, had then held them down the way a cop pins a caught suspect, whose hands itch to reach but can't, had left them there as markers reminding future sorters to revisit the matter. Her stomach sickened as she saw him, the decent priest, the good priest, the kind who didn't have the *sick tick,* sitting in here alone and unsupervised, licking his thumb touching and these secrets, dog-earing some with a code no one knew, signaling God knew what? Christine snapped back to her sorting, spat out her braid's frayed end, nothing to cushion her grinding teeth. She exhaled hard.

The cabinet, which guarded decades of dust, exploded with motes, a whole cosmos of chaos hidden here.

The bishop, his gleaming white hairs like strings of ivory tinged with ebony, his eyebrows architectural arches, his dogmatic smile seeping even through the phone, winning out even over his rash and raised voice, erasing the objections she'd lined up before him like a guest list of important donors he could not refuse:

"…"

"Everything you need to do away with is in the old cook's quarters. The cabinet takes the same key as the one in my office. Use the old stove."

"…"

"Shred or burn them or even bury them if you have to. I strongly recommend the old stove. But the fireplace at my house if you have to

128

dear, the key is under the Virgin's statue, which tilts back real easy. Easily. It should be real easy to do all this. The only difficulty will be doing it in time. At the right time. So as not to call attention to it. Quickly enough. I'm catching the next plane, I assure you."

"..."

"But that's the whole point, hear me. We've been cooperating for years, for decades with the law, and now they're demanding that we dig up the cases of dead men to fit their godforsaken—to, to what? Don't you see? To meet the demands of a sick media theater that unearths souls from graves and parades corpses across the national stage, why, Christine, why? I'll tell you what comes of it: condemn the living to a hellish life ruined—defined—by a past that won't die. To kill the faith. That's what this is about, Christine. This isn't about the abuse, for the newsies. It's a shrewd power play to crush the Church."

"..."

"No, this is not a matter of wrongdoing, of doing wrong. Yes that's the way they want to twist it. They're the ones . . . they're overstepping their bounds. Absolute power to invade even the Bride of Christ. What right does a corrupted state comprised of one too many criminals have to weigh us in the scales of their courts? Absolutely none."

"..."

"Listen to me, Christine, if it'll ease your conscience I can tell you this: I'll be the one who's held responsible for whatever you do. But tell me you'll do it. I just can't come back from Rome in time to beat the—"

"TLAK"

"Oh—Christ!"

Bent at the caesarian scar that cut across her belly, Christine delivered a pained puff of cool gray air in the fireless night—the twenty first of December, darkest day of the year. The papers, though nearly weightless, felt heavy in her hands. *Enough.* With a shove she slid a footrest to the base of the bureau. *There.* On tiptoes again, she managed to grasp a couple of hemorrhaging folders that balanced precariously above the abyss. The key could stay there. But not a single file. The bishop was firm. "One left behind would mean others done away with."

For now her hands held them tight, kept the flattened wings of white paper flightless in her grasp, like the stuffed dove her mother handed her when she was three. A gift from Father before he was bishop. She sneezed. Her mother's job before her: secretary to Father. It had been a good fit. It had been. Ordering the days of the man who had come to see her mother at home, winning smile stale-mated for a long time as he stood there, chest out, hands full of frosted lamb. Met by mother's literal cold shoulder as she paced down the hallway and through the kitchen with the crying Christine, trying—she later admitted, over the margaritas made strong by twice the tequila—to blink away the affinity between the little lamb's eyes and Christine's own, "which, I mean, sweet Christ what a... should've been comforting, but it really freaked me out, really, when he came with that cake, ridiculously sculpted, *crazy*, like a sculpture from the Vatican or something, with all these little peaks of frosting like, like real wool, girl, *crazy!*, licorice for eyes, like your little ones, so pretty you were and are, but then the thing was this. I kid you not. Why it cracked at my head the way it did, does, like something snapped right here"—tip of her index to the side of her temple—"I don't know, but when I blinked and looked again one of the little lamb's eyes had fallen out." And the bishop waited at the door in a bent arc, limbs tangling the shock of dejection and the jittering fervor of prayer, hands folded under the lamb, heavy head hanging like the curled top of a crosier until her mother stopped whirring in circles and turned off the television that had been blaring a game show in the background.

And then the bishop, balancing the cake on a tipsy TV tray

and taking Christine's drooping and near-spineless head into the cleft of his elbow, whispered to silence the cawing baby. Her stunned mother watched him kiss this bastard child, conceived within sin, the one he had talked her out of terminating. Christine's mother had come to him in the confessional and, coughing and reeking of cheap marijuana and double-menthol cough drops, said, at the end, *There's nothing you can do to make me keep this… Father, no f-ing way, see,* staring down the man who blinked and said, "Shhh. Peace. I think I've got a way for the bills to get covered, a little," and proceeded to hire her as his secretary, paying her twice the typical wages. True, in those first years there was no nipple to calm her into the loud and sloppy and happy sucks, but Christine could nestle at rest in tortilla-shell-smell of the nanny Lúcia's cornflower dress. To say nothing of this: Christine grew up outside of the gravities of necessity that would have otherwise been the smithy of her childhood, had it not been for the bishop who had asked her to incinerate the only evidence of things done by hands that, so faith said, turned unleavened into Light.

Christine stared at the two towers of paper that threatened to collapse but leaned against one another like drunken friends clanking their foreheads together. Keeping them there, whispering secrets.

Across the street, in front of the bishop's penthouse suite, the faint screech of bad brakes announced his arrival. The blood red snow now held no body, but police still surrounded the scene, sectioning it off with stretched yellow tape. The Escalade, which he always drove to and left at the airport, needed a tune-up. No. Him here how? Christine kicked the footrest and her toe pulsed with pain. She shoved it again, this time with her shin, and, stepping on it, clamored in the cabinet for a large pan. She found an old stainless steel one with a scorched base, one that had the faint reek of potatoes and leeks gone sour. Soon she was at the sink, cranking the faucet and filling the thing with the rust orange water the pipes coughed up, chunks of crumbled metal lining. And then the flood came. Clear water. Its forceful flow keeping the rust down.

Stretched between two deeds that needed doing, she spied the old purple phone, the color of bad bruises left untreated. Snatching it from the wall, she dialed the police and shuffled back to the sink, the cord barely reaching as she said, surprising herself with the sick sarcasm, "A Christmas present for you at the dioceses. 665 Damien Street. Things with tears in them. Vases and pots and buckets of tears. Bowls and bowls of them uncried." Her voice was melted, mercurial. She tasted metal at the tip of her tongue, which had quickly tired from the words she had *yes* she had *yes* she had said them out loud.

"Ma'am," the dispatcher asked, "could you give me a few more details? We need to know who to send. All kinds of scenes going on tonight. Is somebody hurt? Are you having thoughts of harming yourself?"

(Mind, my mind, please. I'm losing mine.)

"I'm having thoughts of the harmed," she said, "And those who harmed them. And I can't stop having them."

"Ma'am," the dispatcher said, "could you give me your name?"

"..."

"Ma'am?"

"A whole lot of people are hurt here. Too many to count. Some of them long dead. Some look just fine, doing just fine, sure, sure, but they're dying, too. You ever seen the waking dead, sir?"

"You said 665 Damien Street?"

"Yes. Hurry, please. Please. Please hurry."

The massive pot was filled to its pouting lip with water. Eyeing the stove, the rusted potbellied thing that still held forth in the corner like an old Catholic Irishman telling tall tales, she shut her eyes and heaved the container, foisting it up with her thigh, giving her knee the ache of a saint who has prayed for hours unknowingly, sure of his nothingness yet somehow forgetting it, kneeling in the night when the house is asleep.

The water flooded the stove's open stomach, dampening every inch, streaming onto the blood red marble below.

She heard the wooden stairs flinch, heard them suffer under the bishop's steps, which grew bolder as he ascended. And, as he ascended, she confused his clomps with those of her whiskey-wet grandfather, estranged for so long but discovered and taken in by her mother when the choices for him were the streets or worse. And there he was, coming home far after dark and finding her in the kitchen, knitting, sitting there age nine with a plate of yarn he would mistake for spaghetti. He kisses her nose, blowing into it his badly-minted breath, the breeze of the broken and the breaking. Giving her a penny and praying a *Dios te salve.*

The bishop, naked of décor but for his black clerics, ducked and squeezed through the door that seemed made for humans much smaller than those who now walk the earth.

"Christine! I cannot thank you enough, but I will," he said, "I assure you that I will," patting his charcoal-colored vest, ridding his pocket of one scrolling receipt after another until at last he found the matchsticks. "I regret that our last conversation was... hard. Here. Let me help you."

Striking one and holding its thin body before the towering stacks of files, and heading over to the stove, he stepped back, stumbled away as one does to evade the circumference of shrapnel when a bomb blows up. Shrapnel in her husband's shin, a sliver flying into his helmeted face. The match, now a corpse with a burnt head, singed his fingers and he shouted "Ow!" She watched him without pleasure, without pleasure watched him fail to understand why these documents blackened by decades of dumbed sins, stained by so many priests' waking wet dreams, dirtied even by blood from bowels, dampened all with the dank stench of rotted, unwept tears—*why she had wrapped all this in silky red ribbons*. Sick. *Sick tick.*

He peered into the potbelly, following the pipe that was to puff all this pain out through its chimney and blacken the air with residual ache. A cosmos of dust motes burning with it, flames tonguing the chaos to God.

But there would be no burning today. Not unless he went through manually, missing appointments. Conspicuous absence.

The bishop saw the water, still weeping, from the stove's bloated gut. First he gave her a killer's eyes. Then, quieting them into slits, he coughed to cover up the hate. She had backed behind the stove like a bad child, desperate to defer her punishment.

But though he looked at her, looked from her to the potbelly to the piles of files, he could make out nothing. In the temporary chill of the old cook's quarters, his breath fogged his thick black glasses. He took them off and looked ten years younger. Like a fleeing father in the alley, useless though not oblivious to his children's cries, entirely unable to amend with his wife, he went to his other woman.

"Christine. What I've done for you. What in Christ's name are you doing?"

She strained to hear what sounded like a siren but could be a stray dog.

"We have work to do," he continued, putting on a nice little face, shaking fingers through charming hair. "I need a scissors, now. Is there—there is no bloody shredder in this room. I'll—I'll be back in just a minute, dear. I have to carry the smaller shredding machine up here. Or maybe you were planning to rip each file one-by-one?"

"Work of human hands," she said, her mercurial voice like a choked chant.

The soundless siren lights, reeling outside now, reached their stellar sears through the window's necrotic rot, through the charred cloak that choked all these filed-away cases, bodies, souls. Bright blue ovals burned through, dangling on the wall and then falling like what—like overripe figs freed from the tree by the breath of life itself.

Proof of the Immortality of the Soul, with Reference to Beeswax Soap

> In this stinking tavern, for instance, here, they meet and sit down in a corner. They've never met in their lives before and, when they go out of the tavern, they won't meet again for forty years. And what do they talk about in that momentary halt in the tavern? Of the eternal questions, of the existence of God and immortality.
>
> —Dostoevsky, *The Brothers Karamazov*

YOU COULD RUSH THROUGH THE SLUSH, then wipe shoes at the door, yellow mat smiling up at the mouth of the store. Seven Swans' Corner Drugs, you have lugged through dark you went fleet through sleet streets with a head wholly hung, for the wind was a howl milked an *ow* from your mouth as it hit like a fist its great gusts in your face. Duck down in from the storm like a crook on the run feel the fluorescent belly—it swallows you fully. Not quite tears but wet flesh you're a mess banished child yes you sorry and glorious child of our Eve, dry your eyes and behold see a busy pack of seekers, bargain finders sad reminders, and midnight believers. A man in sunglasses suave sweat pants chewing chips—all these sons of organ grinders you dismiss at a glance, grumbling and mumbling that the world's gone to hell yet they think o God surely second comings are at hand, there they stand, in a trance how they wait for a sign, wait in line for a sale to offset mortal fines. A lick at the lottery—*mine!* Look a broomstick-thin man with two packs of cigars bulging out of his chest, pockets fatter than his frame, man he's chewing on his sleeves, stepping up to the clerk who'll be here until close, squinting under the beams that illumine the things that his ma clicked her tongue at as he flicked up his finger. But he still can't quite shake that sharp *tsk* when he sees unclad ladies on the covers of shellacked magazines and the color-code condoms claiming pleasures and ease and he clings, cleaves condemned, to the counter's cliff-edge like a cold-blood-caught criminal on apocalypse eve, feeling heat if you will like a fried nervous chicken with five *bona fide* furies biting after his heels. The cashier is basting it now with dark grease but the thing is so hot that it's ready to burst. Son of Eve shakes his head drops his deck of dead ticks, silver-scratched lotteries, unheard pleas and prayer cards, o Our Lady *Fortuna* you are harsh you are hard, and yet sanguine he grows as he eyes all the rolls all the chances to conquer the cruelties of chance. Like some new Sisyphus he insists "Try again," and again in this game he can't win—it's a sin. As a stressed voice from heat ducts says "Blessed be the stubborn" he returns to the checker half-awake with a grin. And the wheel turns gain and again against the grain, if at first fail you fallout then in failure you'll stay. "Well, sir," he says to the clerk checking texts while the chip-chewing man says "Hurry up, I'm next"—"Well, sir I'd say to the cocksure young soul, 'Ain't nothing like failure makes an ass of a man'" and he gestures to you with a jerk of his thumb and now what do you do but heap coals on his head with a nice new cool smile that you've fashioned of late just to get by in style, to so suavely berate. "Just a few licks, but the losses o the losses how they bitter the palate and pique it with parch." He pauses to look with his nose lifted up like a bride with bad nerves sniffing roses like coke, like the addicts outside doing lines in the snow. COME. T. POPS say the suckers, in seventy-seven flavors. Crumbs of colored sugar wrapped in clean cellophane. But the candy bouquet cannot calm him, he's stalled, how to choose from the flavors seventy-seven in all and the *All* swells his tongue like a comet on a stick like a spherical comet someone caught in left field in a cosmic game of baseball for to stall the earth's end at the close of the ninth when at last the asteroid came to take us from here and to take here from us until new Sisyphus, our best player that year, he surprised us and saved us from the brutal cosmos and he smiled as he caught the hurled comet that crumbled and then passed on the pieces to factory hands who had been out of work in the middle Midlands and they took a good look and knew just what to do yes they cooked that chaos into suckers for you. The way little things wrapped in packages—bright—can keep up our confidence in the dark senseless night. The convenience of it all, the achieve of it all of a packaged sweet peace, of a world wrapped in glimmering plastic for each. "Hurry up, c'mon, dude," says the chip-chewing man whose bad barber has cut something barbarous again, "Hurry up please, I have to get back to my wife," but the thin man don't answer just keeps licking his lips and juts out his elbows with a wink to the clerk. "Hey now, my man, my man let's play again please yes this time I'm going to win, and when I do win I will alms-give right then, God I really gotta cover a multitude of sins. Gimme six scratch offs and a Hoi Polloi Millions," after which he descends into desperate silence. Except for the sound of a dime rubbing hard, scraping out little secrets like a dimestore Da Vinci or a lost could be *artiste*—Michelangelo misplaced— who still needs to chip and to chisel away and to sculpt the eternal at the end of the day. The eyes of the thin man are faux-oracles, the eyes are as empty as the pail that he cleans with—the one-armed janitor who swears he's a vet, who scrapes and wipes stains of so many pilgrim feet, of the hundreds who crawl here to homage *Fortuna*, who fidget as they beckon and reckon with luck. "Look man, c'mon you're shaking dirt on the floor." "Forget it, don't worry about it, we gotta make work, tomorrow's the shift of the one-armed bandit." And when the mild vet who is missing a limb turns Seven Swans' floors into Pactolus gleam as it was after Midas had washed in the stream then he limps out the door sweeps crushed glass from the floor of the earth where the addicts all hide on the right, on the shade side of dumpsters in the drugstore's back yard. But back to the thin man how hollow his eyes like the bucket that hangs from a nail on the wall as though boasting its emptiness, relative pointlessness waiting for someone to put it to use.

Not *divertissement ennui* of exchange tit for tat, no this thin man is here to outstare balding odds who want badly to oust him from his unbuckling bullocks. While he's scratching the itches that cry from the tickets the chip chewing man plays a new lottery as he picks up chic packs of clear plastic balloons, prophylactics, he goes spastic with brags masked as a brood. "Got to keep the woman pleased" he utters repeatedly, adjusting his sunglasses, tweaking his smirk, all agog, all a gag, telling the clerk that he don't need no bag, walks out clutching his brag. But he handed the bills like a doubting clairvoyant who lays out a deck that is worthless with confidence that's summoned by people who charge card their futures. He looked over his shoulder like his bills counterfeit, but the clerk hard at work slipped them into the drawer, making change without altering at all his expressions, then washing his hands in a tiny propped bowl, lacking as he did old Pilate's good lackey who'd prepared the water and toweled off the blood. When the man in sunglasses moseys into the sleet like untouchable mobsters who hired men yet mark, relentlessly stoic as though nothing at all, though mark you he's doubting his chances to take her, asking why did you come on this slush-socked fool errand on this cold mother's eve of the day they call Christmas? Inside *Don Juan* is mocked thoroughly, but somehow the satire only chokes up unease.

Calm down now, man. Come here now, y'all. You could buy a little bar of this there rose soap made of beeswax in China for a dollar or so, crack the cardboard stale shell and let the flakes fall right out, let the little flower scent lift you praise you heavenly hosts, hurry home and let the pumice now purify your pores it has been far too long you are worse than you are, you are less than the lost and the least and the policed, and you've loved to be victim and at once the high priest, you complete all your duties with impeccable speed but you do this to please them and keep all at ease, and then when they scowl or just twitch with a gram's worth of friendly critique how you flee like a fiend into clichéd old pride—no not swear words or blasphemous belches but lies, ecstatically hiding but they're unsatisfied, still you lie and you lie hiding pride, you deny. Go on then. Wrap whatever's left of your soul in the cheap cardboard casing that smells like the roses you gave to a girl, but neglecting to wash out your mouth even once, you've said things, twisted things, charming things just to please and thus charred all the edges of your immortal being, shucking the skeins of your sins so entangled, so spangled with niceness and without real unknotting you buck up a blitheness with just motions and spotlight and the crowd is untruth. And the crowd is untruth. But the skein of your sins still dangles from your soul, attached at the hip and the lips and the head and the good that you did is garbled and gross.

Proof of the immortality of the soul: you let it go without the ablution of absolution for so long, if you let your good skin and your godawful bones get stained for that time-line your body would die of disease but your soul though you've cut it and hacked it into pieces, pulling out this part and keeping quiet compartments—shoving shut all the aspects that could cut short success, though you've fouled it and soiled it like a child in wet sheets who forgets to tell mother that he needs a new pair, and it stays there, the reek, for weeks and for months, until finally the whole house is filled with the smell, but not a single inhabitant notices well, so accustomed man grows to about anything, even hell, even hell, even Devil's damned grinding, even when he is chewing and eating us whole, but you know this I know on some level you see, on some tuned-out but blasting everlasting frequency— you know even then that the soul is not crushed like a masticated meal of the body of Adam, as though this old soul was made only of atoms. You can forge the soul's form but you can't make it formless though you came very close to abyss precipice and the void will mistake you, unmake you quite nicely.

Seven Swans has no restroom and you can't wait til home. In the bathroom in the dark room of the corner parish stop. St. Dymphna's, the patron of mangled mad minds. It smells like fish fry and old sweat reeks like death but the door is unlocked and the basement is open. Here Christmas Eve lines are formed towards the confessional. In the bathroom in the dark room at the end of the line, you look left and right and slip in to relieve. Lock the door and take off your clothes. Disbelief. Scarlet coarse rag you rip off of your pants and crimson colored bar slippery in your hands, scrubbing and slapping displacing the dirt, soaping and elbowing out festered hurt, bloody wounds, pustule rot but the boils they don't dot, cannot mar unseen shape, of the soul you near lost. It is finished. Fingers then feeling the clean of the thing, sweet smelling smile, sheer achieve of the things that can happen in the dark room of the corner parish stop. Emerging from asperges, believing ablutions, hankering for the right rite, the line has grown short, you wait for the place where the priest goes to work. No sleight of hand raised over a body of bones. No stench left behind masked by sweet smelling lies, the reek that still seeps from you—homeless for weeks. You'll atone up the way up at last on a love and I leave you let Him cleave you, believe me my love, in the clefts of the rock He will come back my dove, He will find you He will know you through this immortal day, *Agnus Dei* if you bind me I will find you and say, and say it straight I can't make it, *Domine. Domine, Domine non sum dignus*, Old Father, art Savior shore up this blessed failure whose roof is unclean for the meanest of men: *Sed tantum dic verbo et sanabitur anima mea, et sanabitur anima mea, anima mea, anima mea.*

About the Author

JOSHUA HREN, PH.D. is co-founder and assistant director of the Honors College at Belmont Abbey, teaching and writing at the intersections of political philosophy and literature and Christianity and culture. For many years he served as managing editor of *Dappled Things*, and he is founder and editor-in-chief of Wiseblood Books. Joshua has published numerous essays and poems in such journals as *First Things, Commonweal, America,* and *Presence*; his scholarly work appears in such venues as *LOGOS* and *Religion and the Arts*. Joshua's books include *Middle-earth and the Return of the Common Good: J.R.R. Tolkien and Political Philosophy* (Cascade 2018), *This Our Exile* (Angelico 2018), and *How to Read (and Write) Like a Catholic* (TAN 2021).